W9-AND-878

The Life History of a Star

The Life History of a Star

Kelly Easton

SIMON PULSE

New York   London   Toronto   Sydney

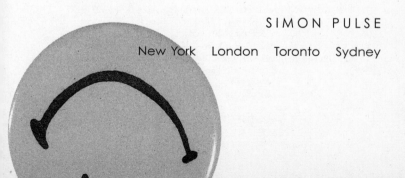

If you purchased this book without a cover, you should be aware that this book is stolen property. It was reported as "unsold and destroyed" to the publisher, and neither the author nor the publisher has received any payment for this "stripped book."

This book is a work of fiction. Any references to historical events, real people, or real locales are used fictitiously. Other names, characters, places, and incidents are the product of the author's imagination, and any resemblance to actual events or locales or persons, living or dead, is entirely coincidental.

First Simon Pulse edition October 2002

Text copyright © 2001 by Kelly Easton

SIMON PULSE
An imprint of Simon & Schuster
Children's Publishing Division
1230 Avenue of the Americas
New York, NY 10020

All rights reserved, including the right of reproduction in whole or in part in any form.

Also available in a Margaret K. McElderry hardcover edition.
Designed by Michael Nelson
The text of this book was set in Garamond.

Printed in the United States of America
2 4 6 8 10 9 7 5 3 1

The Library of Congress has cataloged the hardcover edition as follows:
The life history of a star / Kelly Easton.–1st ed.
p. cm.
Summary: For more than a year, fourteen-year-old Kristin uses her diary to record her confused thoughts about the physical changes brought on by adolescence and the emotional strain on her family of living with the "ghost" of her beloved older brother who was physically and mentally destroyed while serving in Vietnam.
ISBN 0-689-83134-X (hc)
[1.Brothers and sisters–Fiction. 2. Family life–California–Fiction. 3. Vietnamese Conflict, 1961-1975–Veterans–Fiction. 4. Diaries–Fiction. 5. California–Fiction.]
I. Title.
PZ7.E13155 Li 2001
[Fic]-dc21   99-046910

0-689-87116-3 (Simon Pulse pbk.)

For Arthur, Isabelle, Isaac,
Randi, and my family

✦

PART I

Year: 1973

Name: Kristin Folger

Age: 14 (but feel like I'm 50)

Address: 4175 Mauna Loa Street, Glendora, California (also known as the sweaty armpit of the universe)

Height: Who cares

Weight: Under

Hair: Nondescript brown

Eyes: The same

Best Friend: Carol, and Simon (when he's in town)

My ex-English teacher, Miss Colandra, gave me this journal last semester. Keep track of your thoughts, she told me, they're really quite unusual. Yeah, right.

April 3, 1973

It's the little things in life that get to me: TV dinners; boring teachers; pompous cosmetics clerks; packages of mustard and mayonnaise that only have enough for one bite of a sandwich; fairy tales that end in marriage; cheapskate ice cream clerks; lockers that stick; black-and-white gym suits; the Mod Squad . . . I could go on and on.

April 4

Mom yaps to her friend on the phone about the lateness of my "development." I try to explain the benefit of looking like a boy, the gift of invisibility. Girls are subject to all amounts of attention. My best friend Carol dresses in the frilliest clothes imaginable and has to put up with sweet remarks from just about everyone.

Spent the day at garage sales looking for a birthday present for Dad. Pretty difficult task since the garage sales in my neighborhood are filled with the most unbelievable junk known to man: dusty wicker baskets, blankets covered in cat hair, broken hi-fi equipment, plastic flower arrangements, scratched records. This is what happens when you live in a poor neighborhood. Nothing but junk at garage sales. Finally, Mom had mercy on me and agreed to take me to Kmart so I could buy Dad something new. But first I had to sit in the dressing room and do my homework while she tried on blouse after blouse after blouse (then didn't buy any). I didn't want to get Dad the typical boring present: Old Spice, soap on a rope, bathrobe. I lucked out, though; there was a big sale in sportswear and I managed to get a really nice Dodgers jacket. In a rare fit of generosity, Mom paid the tax.

I hope he likes it.

April 5

Dr. Alger was going on and on about the Big Bang Theory, much to everyone's boredom. I believe in the Small Fry Theory. I think the universe started not with a big bang, but with some tiny organism who was enough of a fighter to continue against the odds. Out of this organism grew the universe. I didn't share this with Alger, though. He got mad enough when I told him that a balanced ecosystem leaves no room for creativity and individuality. The top of his head turned practically purple and he ended class with the following cheerful statement: "One day, billions of years from now, the sun will collapse on itself and that will be the end for everyone. Keep that in mind when you're having your next adolescent crisis." You gotta laugh!

Still, the class gets under my skin. Last night I dreamt of the sun exploding, of Agent Orange and land mines.

P.S. *Pioneer 11* launched to explore the vast fields of Jupiter.

April 6

Woke up late and rushed around looking for my anatomy book. I must've left it in the dressing room at Kmart. I dread telling Mom about it because she hates doing the least little thing for me.

Due to his sickly pathetic health, my dear brother Bobby has managed to get out of PE. Just because he's in high school, he gets to do what he wants. God! What I wouldn't give. PE was cooked up by jocks who want to punish intellectuals like me. I mean . . . every time that volleyball comes at my head—I DUCK— who wouldn't? Because of my superior instinctual response, no one wants me on their team. There's nothing like standing on the pavement watching person after person being called to a team until you're the very last one. Might as well be the last one on earth. Reminds me of that *Twilight Zone*: When a woman has the bandages taken off her face, she is beautiful. Unfortunately for her, everyone else looks like pig mutants and she's the outsider.

When Bobby came home I told him I'd kill to get out of PE. "You wouldn't want my asthmatic lungs, Kris," he said, puffing away on a cigarette.

Called Grandma about twenty times. No answer. Since she hardly ever goes out, I'm worried that she's dropped dead. I wouldn't be surprised. She has clogged arteries, a polluted liver, and dentures.

April 7

Dad's birthday went off pretty well yesterday. Bobby got him a power saw that he must have saved up for for about five months. Mom got him a fancy bottle of scotch, which everyone knows is for her. Dad made a big deal out of smelling it and savoring it and everyone got a taste (tasted like cologne). The big hit was the Dodgers jacket. Dad said it made him feel like he was back in high school. Then he went on and on about his bald spot and being middle-aged, which was really pathetic, and just about the time he's cutting the cake, we hear the ghostly sounds coming from upstairs. Everyone freezes like it's a photograph. Then we all talk real loud and pretend not to notice (as usual). But no one really touches their cake after that and the party breaks up.

April 8

Just finished reading *A Wrinkle in Time* for the third time. It's a kid's book but I like it. In the end, it's only love, not science, that can save them. Like the Beatles song, "All You Need Is Love." Unfortunately, no one has quite figured that out yet.

April 9

Pablo Picasso died. Simon will be devastated. I'm pretty sad myself, even though a lot of his art looks like a kid painted it. It says something for him that he could keep up that kind of spirit even though he was so old.

I miss Simon. He's my only male friend. But since his dad got the position at the university, Simon thinks he's better than me.

P.S. I thought up a new replacement for the Big Bang Theory: the Squeaky Fart Theory. The universe started with a squeaky little fart. Like the last gas of an old man, it stinks for a while, then dissipates into nothingness.

(This is the kind of thing I come up with when I'm down.)

April 10

Mom finally took me back to Kmart for my anatomy book, only to find out that some creep had drawn unsavory (to use a vocab word) additions on all of the skeletal illustrations. I showed these to her and she threw this huge fit at Kmart. The assistant manager assured her that none of his employees would do such a thing, but I saw one of the employees, this really pimply kid, giggling behind the stand of batteries and flashbulbs. The assistant manager offered Mom a $5.00 gift certificate. That placated her. She was even kind enough to give me half; it was *my* anatomy book, after all. I got a couple of really cool Peter Maxx folders, so the day wasn't a complete bust.

Later: Called Simon to offer condolences about Picasso. "He's in his room with the lights out and won't speak to anyone," his mother said. "But he'll perk up; his dad is taking him to Spain so they can both grieve in style in Picasso's homeland." I feel for him, of course, but there always seems to be some reason why Simon can't come to the phone.

April 11

Mom has been bugging me about bleaching my mustache and dressing like a girl. It's a very faint mustache, just a bit of peach fuzz dipped in chocolate milk. She even tried to get me to buy a bra, like I need it!

Later: Mom and I had one of our usual arguments because I wouldn't eat the gray casserole she called dinner. Everything she makes tastes like salt and lard. When she looked at Dad with this mournful "What are we going to do with our daughter?" look, Dad could only stare at the Hamburger Helper and shrug. Then, she started yelling about how nothing was the same anymore, as if *that's* our fault. She is the world's biggest blamer and every time she and I get into it, Dad ends up in it, too. Bobby stayed invisible. As usual. As far as brothers go, I could do worse. I just wish he would make himself more present. If he had been the small fry that started the universe, civilization would have ended right then and there.

P.S. Grandma is okay, but apparently fell asleep under the hair dryer so she didn't hear the phone.

When I told Mom that maybe Grandma was dead in a heap, she said, "That's all I need." I should show Mom the definition of "narcissism" in my psychology book. She fits it to a T. All she thinks about is herself.

April 12

Called the Peace Corps to see if they could assign me to a scenic place like Biafra or Bangladesh. I figure the Peace Corps would appreciate my kind of energy. At first, the woman on the phone sounded interested, especially after I mentioned my experience in engineering (I didn't tell her that it was only hooking up some wires on a CB radio with my dad), but after I exposed my age (I lied and told her I was sixteen), she got all mushy and condescending about the "idealistic youth" and how the world starts in my own neighborhood. I should call in two years (meaning four), she said, and blah blah blah. Finally, I hung up on her, but I feel really bummed out. Here I want to do something useful and, as usual, my efforts are thwarted. I don't know. I vacillate (another vocab word). On some days I feel like I want to do something for the world—something important. I wouldn't tell anyone but you this because it would hurt my image, but . . . I haven't lost all hope. I mean, there are days when the idea of some little kid not having books to read or somewhere decent to go to the bathroom makes me want to devote my life to service. But other days, walking down Alosta, observing the scrawny deadbeats and disappointed housewives with their dangling cigarettes and beer breath—well, this is human reality and it just makes me want to push the button myself. The human race is a disappointment. We need to acknowledge this in order to improve. The animal world is more respectable. Did you know that if an elephant falls, the rest of the herd won't abandon it? I mean, it could break a leg and the others would stand right by it. Whales, in their amazing migration, take the very same path to spawn each year, traveling thousands of miles to Baja. Loggerhead turtles scurry from the ocean to the beach to lay a hundred eggs, even though most of the babies will never make it to the sea.

April 13

Carol and I are growing apart. She's my best friend, but she's changed lately. Yesterday, she got in a fistfight with Nancy Jennings about a comment Nancy made to Gloria Denim about Carol's father acting like a caveman at the baseball game. Carol wants me to ambush Nancy in the bathroom, but I told Carol to forget it! #1, I'm a pacifist. #2, It's too pathetic—I mean, Nancy is one of these girls who end up cranking soft serve at Dairy Queen or winding the laces around the skates at Ice World for the rest of their lives—I just wouldn't have the heart. Plus the whole thing is totally convoluted; everyone knows that Carol hates her father's guts. So what's the big deal? He *is* a caveman—and a pig. Still, the whole thing got me thinking about that "man versus man" stuff that English teachers are always going on about. I asked Bobby about this, but his idea of rebellion is peeing in the swimming pool or cutting the "do not remove under Penalty of Law" tags off of pillows.

I wonder if Simon's in Spain yet.

April 14

Found an interesting book about some lady's childhood in France. See, her parents ignore/don't understand her, so she forms this intellectual life-of-the-mind thing. It's called *Memoirs of a Dutiful Daughter,* by Simone de Beauvoir.

April 15

Mom and Dad are having a nervous breakdown together and, as usual, are filing an extension on their taxes. When Dad gets freaked out about finances he goes into the garage and invents gadgets. His latest is a contraption that opens jars. I think it's kind of pointless to invent a complicated gadget to do what can be done simply by the human hand. Dad has things reversed a bit in this sense; his creations make things more difficult rather than easier. Still, he enjoys it one heck of a lot, so I'm not going to butt in.

Meanwhile, Mom is on a determined kick to "reduce," so the rest of us are stuck drinking pale watery milk, salads covered in vinegar and lemon, raw carrots and salted celery. Yum. She drinks about twenty diet sodas a day and calls this a health food diet. You don't have to be Einstein to figure out that consuming that many chemicals a day will pickle your organs, not to mention the amount of vodka and bourbon that she adds. Naturally there are no more cookies, cakes, chocolate milk, etc. available. Her rationale? "It'll do us all good." Even Dad knows to head for the garage when she starts in on that line.

Bobby's been bugging me to play a musical instrument. He's learned to play the guitar really well and says that family groups are in these days. I can just see us: the next Osmonds. He's such a dork, but it's hard to get mad at him. He has such a pitiful look on his face when he fiddles with his glasses. He looks twelve, not sixteen. Still, I hate myself for being such a softie. Anyway, I told him that I would try to talk Dad into getting a piano or something.

Carol's father, the fascist, caught her smoking and made her smoke cigars until she threw up all over the lime green shag carpeting. Carol's mother, Tracey, was furious. She said she worked all summer just to pay for that nice carpet. Tracey kicked the basset hound, which was asleep and didn't notice, but Carol's dad loves the dog, so he hit Tracey in the mouth and knocked out one of her teeth. Nice, huh? I feel sorry for Carol. Even though my parents are neurotics, they draw the line at kid and dog abuse.

April 16

Ghost howling all night. There's nothing scarier.

April 17

Dreamt I had joined the Peace Corps, but instead of sending me to Bangladesh or India, they sent me to downtown L.A. I'm in L.A. and the Peace Corps lady tells me to erase graffiti. But I thought I was supposed to help people or teach English or something, I say. "No, your job is to erase. . . . You shouldn't underestimate the importance of erasure." So I start cleaning the walls, only it's not the usual language I'm erasing, it's just these words in big letters: SEARCH RELEASE CLING FIND. I clean and clean, but nothing is erased and then I'm in Palm Springs at the Sands motel, swimming in the kidney-shaped pool—and I think: Why shape a pool like a human organ that handles waste? Then my mother appears in a tree and says, "Get out of that pool; your father wants to camp, so the whole vacation is work!" and I say, "I can't. I'm swimming in a pool of tears."

"Kristin!" My mother shook me awake. "You are going to be late for school again and I'm not making up some kind of note this time because the school knows that I'm lying." I wanted to come up with something smart to say, but I could see from the dark circles under her eyes to clam it. The ghost had kept her awake all night, but I'd slept right through it.

April 23

Still plugging away at *Memoirs of a Dutiful Daughter.* I'm on the part where she gets older and sits around

Paris, drinking wine and being an intellectual. Sounds okay to me. There's a philosophy I found out about from it, that sounds like it would suit me to a T: existentialism. It's about how God has done a disappearing act, and existence doesn't mean anything unless you're an intellectual. There's a big emphasis on individuality. The masses are asses, as the saying goes. You have to think for yourself.

April 24

This semester is a totally lost cause. The literature class is a joke. Mr. Causeway spent the whole first week dissecting the hopelessly boring "Stopping by Woods on a Snowy Evening." Causeway insists that the narrator guy isn't bummed, but I think he's gonna off himself with the shotgun hidden in the blanket. He's probably cheating with the guy in the "village though's" wife! If not—what's the point of the poem? And anatomy class is gross! Looking at a bunch of drawings of bones and organs, I just want to scream and run out of the room. Still, it has given me more sympathy for the anatomy teacher, Mr. Spokes, and why he is so petrified (meaning both: scared, and like a rotting tree). Speaking of science, Alger did a real song and dance against the creationists. I almost shared my Small Fry Theory with him, since he's clearly an atheist as well.

April 28

Carol is really bummed out. She says that her father threatened to lock her in the garage without any food and water. I said that her father's fascistic principles were responsible for his behavior. "Is it catching?" she asked. I assured her it was not. I guess it's easy to see why Carol wants to punch in everybody's face all the time.

Had an argument with Mr. Causeway because I don't think the lyrics from Irving Berlin's songs constitute poetry. He said that Allen Ginsberg (my suggestion) doesn't constitute poetry either, even if he *is* included in the Norton Anthology. He also informed me that "Howl" was banned at our school and I can refrain from quoting it. Leave it to our fascist school board to ban great works of art. Even in my dream, I didn't like the idea of erasing: words, thoughts, anything.

April 29

Went to visit Grandma at her senior citizens' apartment complex. I'm really the only one who ever visits her. Mom hates her guts so she only goes on Thanksgiving and Christmas to bring her slices of undercooked turkey and salty boxed dressing. Dad is more loyal, considering she is only his mother-in-law and complains to him about who her daughter ought to have married. He visits occasionally and yells at Grandma as if she's deaf and she yells right back, even though her hearing is fine. Gives me a headache. Grandma was feeling pretty bummed today and, for once, she didn't make me eat, which was a relief because the smell of that place, like stewed prunes, Metamucil, and decay, makes me sick to my stomach. Grandma always blesses me for coming, but it's kind of annoying the way she keeps the TV game shows on full blast the whole time, when I just want to shoot the breeze. Old people aren't all they're cracked up to be. They're supposed to be wise and good listeners, but most of the time they're complainers. The thing I like about visiting is that she lives next to the arboretum. After I visited her, I sneaked over the fence and watched the peacocks for an hour. The bus ride home was full of the usual loonies and retards. You'd think Mom would pick me up! It's *her* mother.

God, I wish I could drive, like Bobby. Then I'd have some freedom.

Later: The coyotes are howling up a storm. An eerie reminder of our ghost. At first, I thought it was an owl. There's not much difference. The owl asks who. The coyote complains—owwho.

April 30

The ghost was moaning all night, so it was hard to sleep. When it first came home, it was stunned and silent; a large rough stone. Lately, it's become violent. I wish Simon would get back from Spain. He's my only real refuge.

Bobby convinced Mom and Dad to buy a used piano. He said it would keep me out of trouble.

May 1

Who ever said "the lovely month of May" was an imbecile. Six weeks left of school. The smog is so thick you could cut it (as Mom would say). The pathetic "Spring Fling" dance is coming, and all the love-struck teachers will drape toilet paper flowers around the gym. Each girl in Mrs. Gammon's home yech class has to fill her quota of toilet paper flowers before she can go to lunch. Mine look really stupid, like everything I do in this boring class. I told the principal that I wanted a course in existentialism. "When you can define it, you can have it," he said, which is dumb.

Everyone knows that existentialism, by its very nature, cannot be defined.

May 2

At the end of world origins class, Alger announced that Eve was black. He said Eve is a scientific name for the common ancestor. All of us carry her genes. This is kind of a cool idea from a humanistic point of view.

May 3

Had to go to school late after being "spoken to," translated "hollered at," by Dad because Carol's dad, the fascist, told my dad that I was smoking behind the AM/PM mini mart, which I wasn't. I pointed out to Dad that he and Mom keep me in the L.A. basin smogland rather than taking me to live somewhere healthy like Oregon or New Mexico. Then Dad replied that the nuclear bomb tests were set off in New Mexico and that all the movie stars who worked there have gotten cancer.

"Thanks for the history lesson, Dad," I replied. Then I told him (truthfully) that I have many vices and smoking is not one of them. Smoking really is gross. You don't have to be a genius to figure out that inhaling a bunch of smoke is going to burn up all the little hairs (cilia) in your lungs. He sent me to school anyway, even though I told him this injustice had demoralized me too much to go. To make it even worse, Bobby walked in just at that moment and pulled out a Marlboro without even so much as a blink from my dad.

Later: Alger came into world origins absolutely purple today. "What's the matter with you people?" he said. "I told you that Eve is a scientific name for a female common ancestor . . . it's not the same one from the Bible—alright? And would you please clarify these things with me before you go tattling to your parents? After all, this is a science class; S-C-I-E-N-C-E, not religion!" Apparently, the bigot types didn't like the idea that they're descended from an African. Really, it's embarrassing living in a country that has enslaved another people. If the thing about karma is right, and you get what you earn, we, as a country, are in big trouble. Like the surgeon said on TV, "Cut them open, and people are all the same." Poor Alger. He was pretty red-faced after that, but he did move on to safer ground, pointing out the differences between categories of prehistoric man in terms of their artistic and mechanical achievements.

* * *

I don't know. Maybe I should be an archaeologist. I could travel to places like Egypt or India and dig around out there until I find something. I would like that—just digging and digging, the hot sun on my back. Ancient civilizations coming to life under my fingertips.

May 4

When Carol went to bite into her bean burrito at lunch, the thing popped open onto the front of her blouse. While the rest of us laughed our heads off, she cried and was allowed to walk home to change. I decided to try that, too, and squeezed and squeezed my burrito but nothing came out. Finally, I opened the thing up, and guess what! Someone had forgotten the insides. Leave it to the school department of "nutrition" to leave out the primary protein source. I think that they are secretly trying to starve us so that they can "decrease the surplus population." Like Scrooge.

Later: Carol came over. She actually *was* upset about the bean burrito incident. I thought she just wanted to get out of school. "Do you know how much effort I put into my appearance?" she said. I just shrugged. I really didn't know. My idea of getting dressed for school is alternating the three shirts I have with the same pair of jeans.

We had a pretty good time, overdosing on popcorn, M&M's, and *Gilligan's Island*. We counted the times the Skipper said "Little Buddy" and laughed our heads off like it was funnier than it really was. Then Mom came and bumped us from the TV so she could watch her favorite show, *The Waltons*. It's a sickening show about this mushy family in the old days. Mom goes on and on about how those were the good old days, even though something disastrous happens every show.

May 5

Mom made me wear a dress to school. Mr. Causeway sent me home, loudly saying, in front of the class, that the dress was indecent. The dress was from two years ago, so of course it was too short. I was totally embarrassed. Mom promised to "raise hell" with the school and have him fired. But I know that she'll never get around to it because she never gets around to anything.

P.S. Causeway makes even President Nixon look good.

May 6

Ordered six cheese pizzas to be delivered to Mr. Causeway's address.

Carol came over and I was going to tell her about my revenge on Causeway, but was afraid she'd blab. We're in some kind of a slump. As kids we used to always be into some adventure or fantasy: building a tree house, selling lemonade, playing James Bond with our Barbies. Now we just sit around, bored. We watch *The Brady Bunch* and make fun of Cindy and Bobby, or *Gilligan's Island,* or *I Dream of Jeannie.*

Out of the blue, Carol said, "They'll be my downfall."

"What?"

"Boys," she said. "I can feel it. I mean, look at Jeannie. All she does is sit around in her little bottle waiting for her master to come home. And he's a big grouch."

"That's television."

"Do you know of any happy marriages?"

I thought about that for a minute. Mostly, the men come home and hide behind newspapers, beers, and cigarettes. "I'm just going to stay away from boys," I said.

"Even Simon?" Carol's always been jealous of Simon.

"Boy*friends*. Not friend boys."

"I won't be able to stay away from boys. They'll be my downfall."

May 8

Put the following ad in the paper: "Found. One brown leather wallet containing $100.00 and no identification. Will the owner please claim." I put Mr. Causeway's phone number in the ad.

Later: Mom must've felt guilty about the Causeway incident, because she asked me if I wanted a new dress for the "Spring Fling." I told her that I wasn't going, but she said I was because she and Carol's mom had plans that night and she can't count on Dad to keep me out of trouble.

May 9

Causeway has been away from school the last two days. Gloria Denim is also missing. Rumor is that she is "with child," as they say in polite society. Not that Glendora qualifies as polite society. This place feels like noplace. It reminds me of the opening to *The*

Twilight Zone, where a clock and a doll and all kinds of other things fly through the dark sky.

I do feel kinda sorry for Gloria. With both her parents being certified retards by the State of California, she doesn't have much of a chance in life.

May 10

Called Causeway's house and, using a Southern accent, said, "Yeah, I heard you people found my wallet. Thank God almighty."

Mrs. Causeway began crying: "HOW MANY PEOPLE CAN LOSE A WALLET IN ONE DAY!"

My parents bought a used upright piano for Bobby's birthday. I wanted a baby grand, but this one sounds pretty good. Mom told us not to play it at night because she doesn't want to wake up the ghost.

I got Bobby a book of piano music at Clayton's music shop. I really wanted to get him the Beatles songbook, but after my splurge on Dad, I could only manage to scrounge $3.95—a combination of my pathetic savings ($1.15), couch digging ($1.15), and pulling weeds ($1.50) for the cheapskate neighbors.

*   *   *

P.S. I feel a little guilty about my tricks on Causeway. I didn't consider the fact that I might bug his wife. She's got enough problems if she's married to him. Really, sometimes it's like I'm a Barbie doll and some great big nasty kid is controlling all of my actions.

May 11

Dreamt that Bobby and I were playing on a big stage with lights flashing on us and that naked people surrounded us, clapping and hooting like mad. It was a big improvement from my usual dreams, where I go to school, and only when I arrive do I realize that I'm naked.

Carol came over and we got all nostalgic listening to Creedence Clearwater records on my pathetic broken-down record player.

Simon is back. He's become a Unitarian and started meditating. Curious things to pick up in Spain. Since he is my only sophisticated friend I'll put up with just about anything.

May 12

When I woke up this morning, I tried meditation. I sat very still, paid attention to my breath, and tried to let go of my thoughts. At first I was bored, like Simon said I would be, but I kept at it. Then I felt pressure on the top of my head. I was weighted to the bed. My mind started zooming, like that arcade game where you steer the car on a swerving road. But my thoughts weren't the spiritual type; they were the ones I've tried so hard to push away. Memories of life before haunting, of life before the ghost, of life before the Vietnam War broke my family into a million little pieces. My stomach erupted like a volcano. I barely made it to the bathroom.

May 13

Bobby's pretty patient about teaching me the piano. He reads music okay, from playing the guitar, and he's picked up the piano like it's nothing. So every day, he sits down with me and goes over chord progressions and melodies, while I try to make my fingers do what my mind tells them to, but they don't want to obey.

May 14

Alger's lecture was interesting: The sea has an influence over our bodily fluids; the tides, the chemicals, everything integrated and only man out of balance.

*   *   *

Going to the Unitarian church with Simon on Sunday. He insists that you can be a Unitarian and an atheist at the same time. We'll see.

May 15

The ghost was up again last night. During the day it's real quiet, probably it looks out the window or watches TV. When it is up at night, Mom gets agitated and drinks vodka.

May 16

As soon as I learn to play the piano better, I'm going to write a rock opera called *Journey to My Higher Consciousness.* I think there can be a higher plane of existence even without God, at least without the traditional guy with the long beard. The first line will be "Journey to my soul, this is my goal." I am going to model it after *The Hobbit* but no one'll know that it's modeled after *The Hobbit* (except Bobby, and he won't tell). I wouldn't want the Tolkien estate to sue me, after all. When I told all this to Bobby, he gave a big smile (he rarely smiles) and said, "I love a girl who thinks big!" He's pretty funny, actually. He always has this look on his face like he's figuring out some complicated math problem, but when I ask him what he's thinking he says, "Nothing. Absolutely nothing."

May 17

Last night a loud, terrifying crash woke us all up. It sounded like someone had driven their car right into our house. It was the ghost. He must've pushed the glass out of his window because this morning dad was outside boarding it up.

May 18

Mr. Causeway is still not at school. I hope I haven't given him a nervous breakdown or anything.

Dad hasn't had a house to paint or a roof to fix for three weeks. When things are like this, Mom gets all hysterical and makes us cheap little dinners like frozen chicken chow mein and canned beef stew.

May 19

Everyone is obsessed with this Watergate business, which looks worse every day. Nixon and his bunch are accused of breaking into people's offices, tapping phones, and keeping an enemy list so they can use the I.R.S. to punish people after the election.

Is it a big surprise that Nixon is a liar and cheater? Mom calls him "Tricky Dick," which is one of the few amusing things she's said in the past ten years. Dad got all pious though: "Innocent until proven guilty," he said, even though he hates Nixon.

May 21

Causeway is back and, for unknown reasons, I was transferred out of his class. The dim-witted excuse was that I would be "more valuable" helping in the counselor's office. This was explained, by the guidance counselor, Mr. O'Neil, as a special privilege. Naturally, I pointed out that this represented a dreadful gap in my education. "Do you want to get into the full details of this, Kristin?" O'Neil asked. He said it in such a way that it was clear I was a suspect. "That's okay," I said.

"Besides, I'm going to give you some books to read and you can write book reports." Something about the way he looked at me made me keep my mouth shut. So I smiled and he grimaced and that was that. Now, I sit in the corner of his office and impress him by reading *The Stranger*, by Albert Camus, and *Nausea*, by Jean-Paul Sartre. *The Stranger* is this totally depressing book about a guy who is kind of mentally separated from himself and who goes out and kills some other guy just for the heck of it. I don't quite get it but I know there is an existential message. *Nausea* I haven't figured out yet either. Just that Jean-Paul Sartre was the boyfriend of the lady who wrote *Memoirs of a Dutiful Daughter* and she thinks a heck of a lot of him. Between reading, O'Neil has me run errands for him. Today he said I was quite responsible, only he said it "response-able" to be clever. There are other benefits of working in the office. While I was filing some papers, the bony secretary asked the gym teacher when Gloria Denim would be coming back to school. The gym teacher winked and said "about nine months," and they both nodded sadly. Guess the rumors were true. I wonder who's the "lucky father"? Yikes!

May 23

ME: Bobby, what are you thinking about? Nothing again?

BOBBY: I'm thinking about my future life.

ME: What about it?

BOBBY: About how I want to live.

ME: So?

BOBBY: You ever think about that?

ME: I used to. So, what do you want your future life to be?

BOBBY: I don't know. I'll be a senior next year. And I get the feeling that I should figure out what I'm gonna do or I might end up just, you know, getting blown around in whatever direction and not having any control.

ME: I'm going to live in Paris and sit in cafés.

BOBBY: Sounds good.

ME: What are you going to do?

BOBBY: I don't know. There's nothing I really excel in, you know.

ME: That's not true. (being polite)

BOBBY: Yes, it is.

May 25

The Soviet Union and America are letting their astronauts train together for a space mission in a couple of years. That is so cool.

May 27

Mom insisted I attend "Spring Fling." Carol's dad put her on restriction for some stupid reason and she had to stay home. My plan was to wave at Mom and hide out in the bathroom until she was gone, then walk down to Jack in the Box for dinner and wander around in people's yards and stuff. Unfortunately, Mom dragged me to school and handed me right over to the home yech teacher, who cheerfully guided me into the dance with ecstatic murmurs about how exciting it is to be young. The teachers think we're morning glories when actually we're thorns. I headed for the bathroom, but Yvonne's gang was in there so I had no choice but to stay at the dance. Chris asked me to dance, probably because we used to hang out in first grade. His idea of dancing is to put his weight on one foot and then the other, like Frankenstein, but without the mobility. He chatted in my ear the whole time. His dad takes him deer hunting in Montana every year, he said, and it disgusts him completely. He's become a vegetarian and dumps his meat into the dog bowl as a protest. Then he started going on about Vietnam, and how it was so sick that Americans went over to kill innocent people, so I told him to buzz off. I hid behind the bleachers picking up junk that had dropped during assemblies: a comb like a seashell, a Tootsie Roll, someone's phone number written ten times in pink ink, gum, a smashed lipstick in orange meringue, a harmonica box, and a five-dollar bill. Simon came in late and pretended that I didn't exist. I asked him what his problem was and he said that he can't relate to me when I'm wearing a dress, so I said, "Then get lost." I hope he'll still take me to the Unitarian church. It may be a place where I can escape on Sundays.

✳   ✳   ✳

Mom and Tracey picked me up. They had gone to a club by the racetrack to ogle out-of-work jockeys; both of them were pretty tipsy. I asked Tracey why she got to go out and Carol had to stay home. She said that she couldn't be responsible for "the brute's" decisions as far as Carol was concerned and that Carol didn't want to go to the stupid dance anyway. The two went on and on about how cute the jockeys are and how one day Willie Shoemaker will come into the club and they'll get his autograph. I said, "What's so interesting about a bunch of short skinny Latins?" They found that just hilarious. "Why surely you know, Kristina, that Latins make the best lovers," Tracey said. Sick! When I got home, Mom and Dad got into a loud fight (not surprising). Bobby came into my room to ask me if I was scared. I think he feels sorry for me. He thinks I'm traumatized, when I obviously am not.

"Guess what? I gave up smoking," he said.

"You deserve a medal," I replied.

May 30

Loved the Unitarian church. No one mentioned God once.

June 1

Bobby and I played Clue and I won. Mrs. Peacock did it with the rope in the conservatory. What the heck is a conservatory anyway? No one has one around here. Just two-car garages. Bobby was too tired out to practice our brother/sister act because he is trying to build up his weakling body by taking a weight-lifting class. He's on some kind of self-improvement kick, I think, because he's also been studying a lot more.

June 3

The music teacher made us sing, "The cruel war is raging. Johnny has to fight." I walked out of the room without permission and thought I'd get in trouble, but when I came back she didn't say a word.

June 4

I guess I wasn't quite out of trouble.

O'NEIL: Mrs. Carrow said you walked out of class yesterday?

ME: That's right.

HIM: Why?

ME: I didn't like the song.

HIM: I see.

ME: Good.

HIM: You have a brother who was in the war, don't you?

ME: Hmm.

HIM: What's his name?

ME: Aren't I supposed to be reading now? I mean, this is my educational time.

O'Neil had me read a story called *The Metamorphosis* by a guy named Franz Kafka. "This is right up your alley," he said. The story is amazing (as far as I've read) and hilarious. It's about this guy who turns into a cockroach overnight. It's just exactly how I feel. My shell is even harder than Gregor Samsa's, even if my insides are still soft.

June 5

Thanks to Franz Kafka, I dreamt of giant cockroaches. Battalions of them, the size of elephants, overrunning the town. Crusty bodies, human faces, like those reptiles from Japanese horror movies. My two brothers and I are perched on a tall building; maybe it's the Empire State Building, because cockroaches are known to inhabit New York. We watch the cockroaches battle each other with swords. "I'm scared," I tell them.

"Let them kill each other off," Bobby says.

"What if they come up here?"

"You don't have to worry, Kristin," David says.

"David," I say. "It's you."

"Who else would it be, little sister?"

"And you're okay?"

"I always told you, don't judge things by appearances."

"But what are we going to do about the bugs?" The cockroaches are getting closer.

"I told you. You don't have to worry because you can just fly." So I jump from the building and it's true . . . I can fly. The city has shrunk to gray and green squares. But, the further I go, the smaller my brothers become. I try to turn around, to get back to them, but I'm out of control and I can't go back.

Ghost *(noun)*
1. A person's spirit appearing after death.
2. Something very slight—as in *a ghost of a chance.*
3. A duplicated image in a defective telescope or a television picture.

Remains, filmy forms, traces, hauntings, holdings, remembrances. David.

June 6

School out soon. Mom wants to take me shopping for clothes. I know what that means: girl clothes. She wants me to be like her, like them. She knows that as soon as I dress like a girl, I'll have to act like a girl. Lose my freedom. Happens whether I want it to or not, like being an actor in a play. Everyone knows that half of acting is the costume. It transforms you. I want to stay me. A boy. Boys act. Girls wait. For what? Boys.

June 7

Went shopping with Mom and actually had fun. She was in a good mood and kept saying, "Oh, this would look so cute on you." Everything that was ruffles and lace. "I'm not three years old, Mom!" I'd tell her, and she would put on a clown frown. I got some really cool platform shoes, a Flower Power T-shirt, and these psychedelic bell-bottoms (that Mom hated)! At lunch, Mom had a glass of wine and became very talkative. She talked about how sour Grandma turned when Grandpa Morton left her and how she felt like Grandma left then, too, "in spirit," so she had to practically raise herself. Mom would sneak out of the house at night to meet boys, "before I learned better, of course," she added. I came away liking her a little more—a danger, since parents are as likely to disappoint you as to pour themselves a cup of coffee in the morning.

June 9

Bobby's in love! I found him on the porch mooning over some pretty dark-haired girl in the yearbook. His glasses were all steamy and he flapped the book closed as soon as he saw me. I asked him to give me a piano lesson, but he wasn't there. He plunked on the keys and hummed, but his eyes were out the window. Who could want this disgusting state of mind? *This* is what the poets are carrying on about? I left Bobby to his mushy daydreams. Sorry to say, but with his bony body (which shows no improvement from weight lifting), zits, glasses, and pale, freckled face, he's not exactly a catch. Whoever this girl is . . . I'm sure Bobby's love will go unrequited.

Later: Mom shuffling papers back and forth. "Every which way I shuffle these bills, I still am unable to pay them." When I asked her where Dad was she said, "Saturn," but he was actually out in the garage building a rocking chair for the neighbor's kid.

*   *   *

Later, I heard them arguing in the garage. Then Mom came in, threw on a red dress and pumps, called Carol's mother and was out the door. Carol was off restriction, so I went over to her house. She said that her dad aims all of his anger at her, rather than her mother. I thought that was pretty perceptive. We also got to talking about Karen Kelly, the redheaded girl who's been made fun of her whole life. But now that she has big boobs, she's the most popular girl in school. Figures.

June 12

Mr. Causeway went into the hospital for gallstones. Gross sickness for a gross person.

I can't wait for school to be out. O'Neil's in a mushy mood. He said what a good assistant I'd been and that he'd miss me. I have a swell brain, he said; all I need is to apply myself. Everything turns into a lecture, I answered. I was actually pretty happy about what he said, since I think I have a "swell brain," too. Then he asked me why it was that I got straight A's one semester and straight D's the next. I told him that it depended on my state of mind. "Yes," he said, "I can see that it does."

June 15

Free at last. Somehow I thought—having the entire day to myself—that I would have something deeper to write—that my unformed thoughts would pour themselves onto the paper. But, no. Maybe my "education" of sitting at a desk for six hours a day has wrecked my attention span.

June 17

Bummed out. Canceled my visit to Grandma. As if it's not bad enough to sit in her smelly apartment and watch game shows, the bus ride is honest-to-God hideous, with every outcast and nutcase on board. My favorite is the man in the kilt who makes the shape of a sexy woman with his hands, over and over. Occasionally, he changes his repertoire and smokes invisible cigarettes, which he relights and puts out. Nice.

June 18

The ghost was beating his stumps against the floor again last night. I went up to his door and my heart was racing a mile a minute. All of a sudden, Mom appeared from nowhere. "Stay away from there!" She pulled me away so hard that I started crying. Instead of saying that she was sorry, she looked at me as if *I* were a ghost, then she slid into his room.

June 19

Simon is taking me to church on Sunday. He also gave me some reading material by the transcendentalists that he thinks I am "ready for." I came this close to telling him where to go. . . .

He's so arrogant.

June 21

Horrible! I give up. I agreed to let Mom take me to JC Penney for a bra. It's totally disgusting, I can tell you, a real dirty trick. Overnight, I have grown a couple of boobs. Mother gushed, "Oh! It's finally happened. Oh, aren't you relieved, at your age! I thought it would never happen! Oh, God, soon you'll be bleeding." I wish the ground would swallow me up. As sure as God made little apples (my mother's favorite saying), I will be like them, like females. Anything but that. But it is happening.

"The blood will flow," she says proudly. "You must be the last girl in your school, but it's coming." Gee, I can't wait. I've heard my friends complain that their mothers try to pretend that the "facts of life" do not exist, but I'll tell you—anything would be better than this oohhhing and ahhhing over the banal changes of the human body. "Oh, I'll have to show you how to use tampons; they're the greatest invention to woman." My mother acts like the queen of England is coming for tea. Despite my lack of enthusiasm, I agreed to let her take me to buy the bra. I made myself a promise to keep the sarcasm limited and be a good sport. I also suggested we have lunch at Howard Johnson's since I know they have cocktails; Mom's always a little more agreeable after a couple of stiff ones.

June 22

Saw Gloria Denim at Penney's. In the baby section. Her mother was with her, looking happy as a clam. Gloria saw me and stepped behind a clothing rack, so I figured she didn't want to talk to me. I waited 'til she was in the checkout and yelled real loud, "Hey Gloria, where you been the last nine months?!" Gloria looked like she could die, but her mother, who is certified a retard by the State of California, cheerfully dragged Gloria over: "Oh look, one of your nice friends!" Parents are so dense! My mother got all googly, too. Even though we'd stuffed ourselves at lunch, she agreed to go to Taco Bell for sodas and "chat." Gloria and I sat in the backseat of her mother's car, which was littered with Coke cans, cigarette butts, and candy wrappers. Gloria sneered at me and said, "So you're finally getting a couple of tits." She's a real class act. At Taco Bell, the mothers, being cute, insisted on sitting at a different table than us. Gloria's mom didn't really seem that retarded. And it actually wasn't so bad because after about five minutes of glaring at each other, I surprised myself and said, "Sorry for yelling that at you in the store."

"It wasn't any picnic," she said, "and I don't need to be reminded. I was in Sacramento, which is gross, and was in labor for about a million hours. I had a horrible time." I asked her what she named the baby. She said she gave it away to her aunt who couldn't have kids, and her aunt named it Harriet. The baby came two months early and is still in the hospital. Gloria got to peer at it through a window, even though she hates its guts. When I asked about the father, she said, "I'll take that to my grave." It sounded like a B movie—I'll take that to my grave.

Home now, locked in my room. I tried on the stupid bra, which looks like a giant Band-Aid, then started reading *Jane Eyre,* one of the books on the reading list for high school. It's about this meek little governess who focuses all her attention on men.

All quiet up above, for once.

I'm glad, 'cause I feel kind of worn out and sad.

I wish that a magnet would draw me through the sky as far away as I can go—to the moon, out of existence, or even farther.

June 23

Started bleeding. Gross. I hate it when Mom is right and I hate this more than I can possibly say.

Later: No one to talk to. Bobby's not home. Carol's family went to Yellowstone. Simon is at his course in hieroglyphics at the museum. I thought of calling O'Neil but don't want him to get the wrong idea.

June 24

I thought I'd try to get a look at the ghost, maybe talk to him a minute or two, but Mom kept going up there with food, clean towels and stuff, so I had to lay low. Bobby rolled up his sleeves and showed me his new muscles. "What do you think? Can you see a difference?" he said.

"I guess so, but don't you think it's weird to have

muscles without really doing something like work or a sport?"

"Oh, lifting weights is work." He pushed his glasses up on the bridge of his nose. "Somehow, I don't really look like a rock star, though."

"Well," I said, "you just stay in the background and I'll stand up front with the microphone."

"Like Karen Carpenter?"

"Too sweet."

"Grace Slick?"

"Too tough, even for me."

"Tina Turner?"

"No. Too energetic."

"Diana Ross?"

"Perfect," I said, then I did my imitation of "Stop! In the Name of Love," sticking out the palm of my hand like a crossing guard. Bobby laughed his head off, which was not exactly the effect I was after, but oh well. I'm downright desperate for *any* kind of attention. It's pathetic.

Cramps.

June 25

Rode my bike to Winchell's Donuts to meet Gloria. We had a pretty good time. She hates just about everyone and makes hilarious impersonations of her retarded parents. She's the funniest person I know. When I told her how depressed I am, she said, "Are you on your period or what?"

"Yeah," I said.

"Well, that's why you feel that way."

"Sure. I knew that."

I guess I didn't. Mom never mentioned that part in her litany.

Carol came back from Yellowstone a week early. Her dad hit her mom in the face while they were driving and Tracey jumped out of the car, leaving Carol and good old Hitler/Mussolini to drive back together. Poor Carol. She was so terrified that she just huddled in the backseat while her father ranted. He drove straight through, so she didn't even get a smoke. It must've been hell for her; she's a total addict chainsmoker. At least my parents are just neurotics and sociopaths; Carol's dad is a total psycho!

I told C. that she needed to transcend her parents' ugliness with higher thinking. "It's no use," she said. "I flunked second and fourth grades because I didn't have enough brains, and now, nothing is changed. Besides, Mom is pretty, not ugly."

"She should leave him."

"She says we couldn't afford to live on our own. He actually makes pretty good money restoring those old cars and stuff."

Later: Sudden panic at the idea of starting high school.

I feel kinda lost without O'Neil. Who's gonna tell me what to read? I looked up O'Neil's number and called him at home. He was sleeping, he said, but agreed to talk. He eased my fears by telling me that it was my high school grades that counted for getting into college. "But," he lectured, "you'll need to—"

I cut him off. "Go to bed, O'Neil," I said. "Don't lose any sleep over me." Just as he was about to hang up, he said, "Don't think you're gonna escape me or my lectures, Kristin. I've been transferred to Glendora High." My heart was pounding for some reason then.

July 1

I can't believe it. Carol has a boyfriend. Freddie. She drags him everywhere we go. He lounges on top of whatever piece of furniture is available, drags her toward him while she giggles, sucks on her neck like a vampire, leaving hickeys. Classy. If I weren't so desperate for company in this boring summer I would tell them both to get lost. Gloria is in Sacramento visiting the baby. What I wouldn't give to go somewhere—anywhere: Morocco, India, Greece. I'd even settle for San Francisco or Palm Springs.

July 2

Spent the day practicing rock-'n'-roll moves in my room to Ziggy Stardust. Bowie is way cool, but I'm way clumsy; I somehow doubt that our brother/sister act will take off.

July 4

Mom went to San Francisco with Tracey.

Happy Birthday, Mom. Happy Independence Day, America, country of bad taste and meaningless wars. Happy "independence" day, ghost. You who've lost yours.

July 10

Am trying to force myself to write, but things are worse than ever. The ghost never sleeps now; there isn't a moment we can forget him. So many of the stories I thought were frightening—Frankenstein, Dracula, Jack the Ripper—seem like nursery rhymes.

Life sure isn't John-Boy and the Waltons.

July 11

Saw Simon at Baskin-Robbins. He stared at me as if I were a creature from another world. I started talking to him, but he just sat there with his mouth open. "What's the matter with you?" I asked. "Didja have a lobotomy or something?"

No answer.

Everyone's weird this summer.

July 13

The ghost had a tantrum and smashed the mirror in his room and knocked all of his trophies down.

July 17

Carol and Freddie spend all their time drinking Annie Green Springs wine and putting their tongues down each other's throats. I bet Freddie uses pot because I heard C. telling him that I didn't approve of it. Why they need an audience is beyond me. Everything I say strikes Freddie as funny. He leans his head back and says, "Whooaa, you are such a trip, Kristin, such a trip. Isn't she a trip, Carol?"

"Yeah," Carol says, "Kris is really a trip, didn't I tell ya?" Ugh! But, really, what are my choices? Goody-two-shoes, cheerleaders, hoods, or . . . the in-betweeners and outsiders. I remember Freddie from Bidwell Elementary; he always had a runny nose, pants that were too short, and a strung-out mother. If there was a kid who wouldn't have his Halloween costume, or his permission sheet signed, it was Freddie. Can't blame him, I guess. Maybe something's wrong with me, but, somehow, the idea of spending hours exchanging saliva with some adolescent guy doesn't strike me as an interesting way to spend the day. Besides, most of the girls I know (like Gloria Denim) who have had sex describe it as being like having a dentist stick his hands in their mouth.

July 19

Freddie offered me a ticket to the Rolling Stones concert, but I said, "No, thanks." Crowds really give me the heebie-jeebies, plus I don't see what's so great about Mick Jagger. His body looks like a skinny ten-year-old's. His dancing with the microphone is creepy, and his lips remind me of those wax lips that people always stick in my Halloween bag. Yech! I'll take John Lennon any day, the rock star of the intellectuals.

July 21

Bummed out. I'm like a pathetic human specimen

who will never be able to fit in to the functioning "normal" world. Through a series of genetic and environmental mishaps, my life was over before it began. Not only that, I've become really fat. As if overnight, all of my clothes are tight and uncomfortable.

Later: Reading about suicide; women are less successful than men at killing themselves. Men use much more effective methods: blowing their brains out, jumping from tall buildings. Women tend to take drugs or make inefficient slices on their forearms, missing the veins completely.

Later still: Mom just came in. She sat on my bed and looked around the room. She kept wiping her face. Then she said my name a couple of times. Just to end the awkwardness, I told her that all of my pants are too tight. "You'll be okay in a few days," she said. Then she walked out.

July 27

Back to fitting into my clothes and feeling a bit better. This period business is just peachy keen. "Are you telling me that I'm going to spend one week out of every month feeling fat, tired, and suicidal?" I asked

Mom. She pulled her dried-up meat loaf out of the oven and said, "Uh huh." If I believed in God, I would tell him off right now for *that* little trick. Dad came in, took one look at dinner, and went to the garage. Mom slammed around the kitchen for a while, then served me about two tons of the disgusting meat loaf and herself about a spoonful (reducing again). She sat and watched while I ate the stuff. Each bite made me feel more and more like I was gonna puke. I knew better than to complain. Mom's anger could part the Red Sea.

Bobby wasn't at dinner. He has a new girlfriend. Her name is Michelle. She's the one from the yearbook! Just when I started getting used to him, he disappears.

Every time I see Simon, he acts all weird and tongue-tied. You would think that world travel would mature him a little. I miss spending time with him. I even miss his mother. She acts like she's about fifteen rather than forty and makes all kinds of exotic foods like artichokes and guacamole, or orders out. I haven't eaten dinner with them in about six months.

August 1
Mom and Dad would like to blame the ghost for their marital failures. They use words like "stress" and

"strain." I think the words "stubbornness" and "nasti-ness" fit the bill a little better. Are there any adults who want to take responsibility for their lives? I think they're a bunch of blamers. Mom mentioned "marital counseling."

"Over my dead body," Dad said, which means he'll end up there. I don't know why, but I feel sorry for him. After Mom stormed out, he joked about Bobby being in the clouds. Then I went with him to the garage and helped him sand the seesaw he built for the twins on the next block.

August 4

It's hot as a barbecue. The smog is pressed against the foothills so that you can't even see them. Everyone is irritated, but no one argues because no one can breathe. I laid on the couch in my bikini and watched *His Girl Friday*. I have decided that I will be a journal-ist like Rosalind Russell (in the movie) and not take any flak from anyone unless they look and act like Cary Grant.

Later: Mom has made an appointment for, get this, family therapy. I just want to barf. "Why not go to an AA meeting instead?" I asked, and she would have slapped me in the face if I hadn't run out the front door. I spent the night at C.'s to let Mom cool down. The truth hurts.

Carol and Freddie spent the whole night necking, smoking pot, and listening to Led Zeppelin while I read these stupid rock-'n'-roll magazines in the corner of the room. Tracey and the fascist had gone out to try to save their own pathetic marriage.

August 6

Mom cornered me: "I realize we're all under strain (that word again), but I do wish that you wouldn't feel compelled to attack me all the time. There is nothing wrong with social drinking and I'm sure you noticed that Tracey and I haven't even been out in about a month."

Later: I practiced the piano, but Bobby seems to have cooled off on our act since taking up with Miss Priss.

August 7

Anyone who takes one look at Nixon can tell he's up to no good. His eyes are tiny and his mouth twitches. Still, I am sympathetic to the fact that he grew up in Southern California. No one who lives here turns out right. How could they? Now, if he'd grown up in Vermont, tapped maple trees, snowshoed, and cross-country skied, he might have ended up wholesome.

August 8

Carol had sex. She told me this in the bathroom at school with the water running so no one could hear. I asked what it was like. She said, "Well, you know how when you watch *The Flintstones,* Pebbles has this thing in her hair?"

"It's a bone, Carol."

"Yeah, well boys have their things and when I felt it, I thought of that bone in Pebbles's hair, 'cause it was the size and shape of that. And he puts it in you and it hurts the first time. Then the second time, it hurts less."

"And that's it?"

"Far as I can tell," she sighed.

I sighed, too. What's a person to say?

"What if you get pregnant?"

"It would be an honor to have Freddie's baby."

And we wonder why the world is in such a mess.

August 10

D day. Family therapy tonight. Since Bobby has

this girlfriend he's been pretty scarce, but Mom told him he'd better show up, or else.

Later: I'm home. Ran about eight miles from "family therapy" to get here!

We walk in and there's this short bald guy with glasses grinning and nodding at us. He looks like a little Buddha, except stupider. *Family* therapy is also a lie since clearly *I'm* the only one who's being therapized.

THERAPIST: Do you know why we're here?

ME: We're here to blame all of our problems on a ghost, only with a witness.

THERAPIST: A witness?

ME: You! (I almost said "You, stupid.")

THERAPIST: So you think you're here to blame all your problems on a ghost?

ME: That's what I said.

THERAPIST: That's very perceptive of you.

ME: Or maybe we can just blame them on me as a second-best choice.

MOM: Kristin!

DAD: Let her answer, why don't you? Aren't we supposed to just let it all hang out? Isn't that why we're here?

THERAPIST: Why do you call him "a ghost"?

ME: That's what he is.

FATHER: His name is *David*, Kristin, and you know it.

MOM: He's still our David. He just needs time to adjust.

ME: Three years?

MOM: Two years . . . and a few months.

THERAPIST: How about if I just talk to you one at a time and the rest of you listen? (He beams at Bobby, who's fiddling with his glasses and keeping his mouth shut.) Right now I'm talking to Kristin and I sense that Kristin has a bit of anger. (By this time I'm starting to feel really terrible. It's like when I meditated, a volcano in my stomach.)

DAD: Oh, this is getting us far.

MOM: You won't even give it a chance.

ME: Can we go now, Dad?

THERAPIST: It's a great sign that you've all come here— a sign of not only your present health, but the health of your future relationships. Now, I have a theory that in order to move along we should all try to use the same language. I also feel that this language should be based on our collective sense of reality. (Even Bobby rolls his eyes, while Mom looks enraptured.)

ME: What's *that* supposed to mean?

THERAPIST: That we should choose our words carefully, in a way that clarifies rather than confuses.

ME: You mean me, right, when you say "we"?

THERAPIST: (self-satisfied grin) Thank you for clarifying that point, Kristin. I did mean you at that very moment. And what I hear you saying is that you feel the focus will be averted from the present communications—

ME: I said we're here to blame our problems on a ghost. That way—

THERAPIST: (interrupting me) He's your brother. I want to hear you say that—

ME: (interrupting right back) THAT WAY we won't have to acknowledge the fact that—

THERAPIST: We agreed to call things what they are—

ME: YOU agreed. Why do you say "we" agreed, when only you did? And we are not talking "things," we are talking about ghosts!

THERAPIST: We are talking about your brother.

ME: My brother died in Vietnam.

THERAPIST: No. He didn't.

ME: Yes! He did!

THERAPIST: Kristin . . . I think we can make progress here, but we can make progress here more quickly if we deal strictly with reality!

ME: My brother died in Vietnam. If he's sitting up in the lousy attic, then why the hell am I never allowed to see him?

MOM: Watch your language, young lady! (I begin to cry.)

BOBBY: I think she means . . . probably . . . that is . . . I think she feels that, in Vietnam . . . with the explosion and all . . . that David's soul died.

I'm all blurry then, but I hear my mother sniffling and then they're all talking at once. But I'm remembering how when David was alive, how tight he and I were . . . always planning some adventure or playing some game, and how Bobby was the outsider, the kid who perches on a fence, or sits in the dugout, watching. It was like Bobby was always getting his glasses broken or having an asthma attack. So he became an observer. Bobby's talking in the background, and my dad's got his arm around me. I hear words but they sound indistinct, like when you turn on the tape recorder and it's on the wrong speed. Words jump out at me like in the dream: PROTECT, SEARCH, CONCEAL, CLING. And I remember David, the day that he left. He sat next to me on the porch and fiddled with his shoes: "I don't want to go, Kristin, I really don't. I feel like I'm in some kind of nightmare. 'To serve my country,' and I don't even know what that means. It's like . . . I never imagined that something like this would happen and I would have to go, without anyone asking my permission. But let's keep it a secret, okay? 'Cause I'd like to go on record, if anything happens, I'd like to go on record sort of brave. And if anything doesn't happen, I'd still like to go on record as brave." And he laughed and I smiled and we shook our secret handshake. Inside I was sick, but I didn't know what could happen. What could happen? What could happen to my brother who always came out on top of everything? He might have to kill, I thought; it's likely. Or he could be killed. That would be the worst. Wrong. He could come back missing parts of his body and all of his mind and we'd all listen to him, howling in his room like a wounded animal who needs to be shot and put out of his misery. But no one has the guts to do it.

I bolted. It was like a prison escape, I ran so fast. I took the railroad tracks. When I got here, they were waiting. My mother started in on me right away. "We were worried sick!" she screamed, but Bobby stopped her: "Mom, just let her be." I ran to my room, but she didn't follow. I heard Dad's voice: "Goddamn it! I'm not putting her through that again! I'm not putting any of us through that!"

Everything is real quiet now.

August 11

David. David. David. David. David. David. David. David.

The child questions her mother.

Why did you call me Kristin, Mom?

I'm in love with the letter K.

Why did you call Bobby Bobby?

Someone had to be named after Grandpa.

Why did you call David David?

David is a holy name. A leader of people. A star.

david david david david david david david

David is a holy name. A leader of people. A star. David is a holy name. David is holy. David is holy. David is holey. David is holes. David is absence. David is in holes and halves and quarters, empty places where body should be, empty spaces for soul. Somebody else was sent back instead of David. David is a king. A leader. A star. David is holy. No. David is half divided by hole divided by dead. Equaling nothing.

PART 2

August 17

I took out the charm bracelet that David gave me when I was eleven. It was big then. It fits now. It only has one charm, a little silver unicorn, which looks really sad and lonely all by itself. I remember the day he gave it to me; we walked to the high school and sat in the empty tennis courts. Then we mimed a tennis game. I've never laughed so hard in my life.

August 18

The air is so dry and still and smoggy. My lungs ache. What I wouldn't do for the Santa Ana winds to come and blow this filth away. Even the coyotes are quiet. At dusk they whimper and moan; they don't even have the energy to howl. David has been silent as well. Maybe it's the smog. Or maybe he senses tension in his own ghostly way.

*   *   *

Mom walked into my room without knocking. She spotted the bracelet and went all googly. She remembered when David gave it to me. I asked her to knock next time, but I must be getting more mature, because I couldn't say anything really nasty. I have to admit that I feel for her sometimes when I think about David being "gone," and Dad spending all his time in the garage, so that she does pathetic things like hang out in jockey clubs.

August 20

I woke up at dawn and Gloria and I rode our bikes all over town. There's something amazing about a sleeping city, something that makes the buildings, the windows, the street signs seem to have a secret life.

Later, I visited Grandma. She had made some fudge and it tasted like she'd used a ton of salt instead of sugar. Now I see where Mom gets her cooking skills. Grandma was eating the fudge and didn't even notice when I ran to the sink and spit it out. She went on and on about her first meeting with Morton. He had a flower in his pocket that squirted water in her face, and a pack of gum with a mousetrap in it. She talked about how Mom was such a sweet baby, but became nasty after Morton left on the San Francisco train and never bothered to come back. Then she showed me this list she's making of the events in her "fascinating" life. It was pretty pathetic:

1917: Danced with "the Detroit Girls."

1918: Met Morton.

1919: Married Morton in a civil service. (Was Morton too cheap to pay for a wedding?)

1920: Moved from Detroit to Los Angeles with Morton.

1960: Saw Doris Day in a convertible with her husband, Martin Melcher. Yelled for her to stop and give an autograph but Doris just blew a kiss.

1965: Got to go on *Let's Make a Deal.* Won a washer-dryer and a fur coat. (Yeah, I remember that one—Grandma went dressed as a can of soup. It was the highlight of her life.)

Note that the birth of my mother is nowhere on that list.

I've been thinking about being female. We grow up with all kinds of interests, but drop them for the end all, be all—getting married. Then all of our eggs are in one sorry basket. Simon's mother is the only happy grown-up woman I know, and she's an archaeologist. Simon told me that she spends all her time at the Museum of Natural History looking at bones and old pieces of wood under a microscope. She comes home at about seven, orders takeout, drinks wine, then spends the rest of the evening poring over scientific journals or conducting to Beethoven with a birch twig. This was a complaint on Simon's part, of course, but her life seems pretty good to me, and whenever I see her, she seems happy as hell. Because she has many baskets.

One time, when I told Simon that I admired his mother, he said, "How can you? She wears Birkenstocks!"

Yeah, she wears comfortable shoes like a person who has something better to do with her life than wobble around on high heels.

Later: Called Simon and asked him why he's been so weird all summer. "Surely you must realize that this is a transitional time for all of us," he said, sounding superior.

"Translation."

"Huh?"

"What is that supposed to mean?"

"Uh, it means that you look about ten years older than me," he offered weakly.

"Oh, is that all?"

"Isn't that enough?"

"I thought you didn't like me anymore."

"Oh, I like you, alright."

And here I had a rare moment of weakness. I don't know what's gotten into me. It's like that phrase from the Bible about the left hand not knowing what the right is doing. Parts of me act without conscious choice on my part.

"Please don't stop being my friend," I said.

August 22

Went to church again with Simon. Bobby actually agreed to tag along with us this time. "I need direction," he said.

I really do like the Unitarians. They don't dress up and look phony like they do in other religions. They talk about humanism rather than lies and manipulations of the Bible. Afterwards, Simon came over to my house and we made hot chocolate with marshmallows. Simon said he was planning to streak at a baseball game tonight, as a social protest. He asked me if I wanted to come: "Don't worry, Kristin, it's not that I just want to see you naked. I will only view this in a political context." I told him I'd think about it, which reminded me of my mother, because I knew that I wouldn't go, but didn't say so. I just don't see why I would want to run naked through the baseball field. I should have just told him then and there. He loaned me a book of freak photos by a woman named Diane Arbus; the photos of freaks and retards look like your basic inhabitants of this town. The photo "Woman in Her Negligee" is the spitting image of Grandma. Simon's intention is to be a great photographer—big switch from last year (a great painter). Simon looks down on his father, an art historian and antiques dealer, saying he is merely a tradesman. He's so full of it. His dad has about twenty degrees, teaches a course at the university, takes him to Europe, and looks like a suave playboy. Simon is scrawny and pale, so he's probably jealous. He's such a phony, but I like him anyway.

August 23

Amazingly, Mom agreed with Dad; I won't have to return to therapy with them. Neither will Bobby. I think I scared them by running out of there. Dad didn't get off so easy, though. When he told Mom that he didn't want to go back either, Mom burst into tears and yelled, "Every time I try to do something constructive, there's someone to tear me down."

"I'm not tearing you down," Dad mumbled.

"Then you'll go?" Mom asked in the baby voice she uses when she wants her way.

"If it's what you want," he said.

Case closed.

Later: Simon came over again and carried on about Karl Marx. Simon is always following one fad or another. Then he went on about how active Nixon was in the McCarthy Communist hunt, and how he got elected anyway and blah blah blah. In the middle of this diatribe, Simon stared at me suddenly in this dramatic way and said, "Kristin, don't you feel differently toward me lately?" I shrugged. "You remind me of a wild colt, Kristin, shaking your mane in the wind, running through the open field." Gross! I didn't know what to say. I have a ponytail, so I got the inference, but I feel about as far from being free in a field as anyone can get. "No one will tame you," he said, "but if someone's lucky, they may ride you." Then he sort of lurched forward and kissed me on the neck. I don't know how this relates to Communism, but if you ask me, not at all. Besides, I hate Communism. It was the combination of Communism and capitalism and corruption that killed my brother and sent the ghost back in his place. So I gave Simon a shove and said, "I want the old Simon back, the one who punched me in the face in second grade."

"What's so great about being punched in the face?" He picked up my hand and stroked it.

"You know what I mean."

"Sadly, I do," he sighed. "We're on a different track of sexuality."

"Do you want to play Risk?" I pulled my hand away.

"I have to go, Kristin. I'll miss my violin lesson and my father will have a fit. He's convinced I'm the next Isaac Stern." Yeah, right.

Everyone is going insane. I'd better hold on to my own shreds of sanity as long as possible.

When I feel organized enough to commit suicide, I will first feel compelled to go everywhere I've ever wanted to go. I'll buy tickets on credit (since I'll be dead, I won't have to pay the bills) and travel all over the world: Turkey, Greece, Italy, Scotland, Tibet. By then, I will probably no longer feel the need to kill myself, but because of the large bills I've acquired, I'll have to follow through.

August 24

Simon again. He's very persistent. When I told him my theory about suicide, he said people who commit suicide lack imagination.

ME: What about van Gogh? He had imagination.

SIMON: In art, yes. In life, no.

ME: It takes a certain imagination to cut off your ear.

SIMON: It was only a piece of his ear. Now, if he'd taken off the whole ear, that would be imaginative.

ME: That makes no sense.

SIMON: Okay, van Gogh *did* have imagination; at least he imagined things. The halos he painted around things were an effect of epilepsy on the optic nerve. He really did see that glow. His illness is misinterpreted as interpretation. But that's beside the point.

ME: What *is* the point?

SIMON: Offing yourself takes no imagination at all. What takes imagination is living, and making life beautiful in the face of hideous banalities.

It's just the kind of thing Simon's always saying, but I thought it did make sense.

*   *   *

When he left, he blew me a kiss. It's a gesture I've seen his father do to his mom. Strange. At least he didn't jump all over me tonight.

1:00 A.M.: Woke up to whispers and moans. I went up to the attic. Mom and Dad were in David's room, huddled around the bed. I tiptoed in behind them. It must've been six months since I've really seen him. Mom has given up shaving him and cutting his hair. She's afraid he'll grab the scissors and hurt her. He's gruesome to look at. Dad turned around and yelled at me to get back to bed!

Did you know that people who are close can develop the same body clock? David and I did. I would wake up in the middle of the night, go downstairs, and there he'd be. "You, too," he'd say, then make me hot chocolate and a sandwich. David made the best sandwiches out of the weirdest stuff: salami, anchovies, onions, peanut butter, pickles. "I'm a growing boy," he would laugh. We'd take our feast into the den and look for reruns of *Mission: Impossible* or *The Wild, Wild West*. David loved that kind of show, where the hero is in some kind of trouble but gets himself out by using his shoelaces, or a tie clip, or some other trick. Afterwards, David would clean up so that Mom wouldn't know we'd been there. Once in a while, she'd be looking for something we'd eaten in the middle of the night, and we would smile to each other. Even if Mom had known, we wouldn't have gotten in trouble, 'cause Mom was a pushover for David. Mama's boy, Dad used to tease him.

He was our boy.

August 26

I miss the night walks with David. He knew everything about nature and he loved to talk about it. David believed that trees were live beings who protected us and felt our love. He said that when an evil person went near certain types of birches, the tree would shrivel up and die. He told me all the stories behind the constellations. Cassiopeia was named after the queen of Ethiopia who claimed she was more lovely than any of the nymphs of the sea. Neptune punished her by having the sea monster, Cetus, wage war and destruction through her kingdom. To restore order, Cassiopeia was told to sacrifice her daughter, the beautiful princess Andromeda. He taught me that comets are chunks of ice that have been orbiting the sun beyond Pluto's reach. Halley's comet comes to the earth's realm only every seventy-six years. Wonder where I'll be in seventy-six years!

The tail of a comet can extend millions of miles into space, always in the opposite direction from the sun, blown by the solar breeze. A comet's tail is the closest thing to nothing that anything can be. I love that. The closest thing to nothing.

September 1

Carol came over. She was pretty upset. Her father caught her putting hair from her brush in the toilet and he exploded. He's going to take the next plumbing bill out of her allowance and he actually made her reach in there and pull it out.

Then she went on and on about Freddie. I asked her, What's so great about Freddie?

She said, "He doesn't hit me."

Sad! I flashed on David quoting Shakespeare. *Hamlet* was his favorite play (but he thought it should end with Hamlet and Ophelia escaping together).

"There are more things in heaven and earth, Horatio, / Than are dreamt of in your philosophy."

"Huh?" Carol said.

"Hamlet."

"What are you talking about?"

"There's more."

"More what?"

"More to life than what our parents have, you know? We can do different things than they've done."

"Like what?"

"Like talk to each other at dinner instead of watching TV. Like be rock stars. Like . . . go to Africa and work with elephants."

"I'm afraid of elephants. When I went to the San Diego Zoo, the elephant tried to grab me with its trunk. Then it peed."

"We could become archaeologists like Simon's mom."

"Simon's mom is weird."

"Well, there's got to be *something* higher to look for in life than a guy who doesn't hit you."

"Oh, sure there is. Freddie's really mellow and laughs at just about everything. He tells these jokes . . ."

What else could I say? She's my best friend. We've played together since we were four, but we're as different as night and day. Maybe she won't be my best friend? Now that she has Freddie.

*   *   *

September 2

Bobby likes the church as much as I do. He's even going to drag Michelle.

Dreamed that O'Neil was following me around reciting poetry. Scary.

September 3

Happy Birthday to me. Sweet fifteen.

My birthday is just a reminder that every day I'm growing closer and closer to the horrible and the unimaginable—being one of "them." Carol wears hooker makeup: white lips, raccoon eyes, blue mascara, and dresses like she's about thirty. She smokes and drinks and she's obsessed with Freddie. It's true, Carol's a couple of years older than me, but still, her sexual activity seems like a bad idea. And she doesn't even enjoy it. "I just hum tunes in my head and stare at the ceiling," she says.

Sounds swell.

The mothers encourage our boy madness. When Tracey told my mom about Carol's new "boyfriend," the two of them whispered, then giggled like little children. Gross!

What do they want for their daughters?

Speaking of which, I like Gloria Denim. She had her fill of boys, did she ever. She's the only one who understands my lack of interest in boys. I figured everybody would snub her for getting knocked up, but she's been treated like a queen, proof of what a little fame will do for you.

Dad asked me how I want to spend my birthday. Disneyland? Knott's Berry Farm? "Alone," I said, but I know they're up to something because they've been huddling and whispering. "Fifteen is crossing the threshold," my mother says to me, shaving her legs with her Norelco Pink Power Plus.

"Do you have to buzz that thing while you're talking?" I said.

September 4

My birthday turned out okay. Mom made me a German chocolate cake. Bobby wrote a funny song and gave me a book of Carole King songs for the piano. Dad built me a cool desk with all kinds of little cubbies. It's antique-looking even though he just made it. He even included a locked drawer with my own key, so I know where I'll be putting you from now on. Then I opened the present from Mom. It was a small box wrapped in silver paper, with red, gold, and blue ribbons. She gave me four charms: Virgo the virgin, a musical note, a "K" in an art deco style, and a windmill. Carol came over, and she must have gotten together with my mom, because she gave me a charm, too—a little heart. I wore the bracelet all day, and couldn't really keep my eyes off of it. Mom and Dad were drinking wine and actually talking to each other. Carol was minus Freddie (for once). Bobby plunked out the chords of "So Far Away" and everyone sang, which was really funny because C. has the worst voice of anyone I've ever heard. Ever.

Dad took me over to visit Grandma last night. She didn't remember it was my birthday, so Dad and I didn't mention it. Grandma is getting old, that's for sure. She refuses to leave her apartment because she's convinced someone will "molest" her. Aren't old ladies always going on about being molested? I think it's some kind of pathetic wishful thinking. Anyway, she seemed so much older all of a sudden. That's how it happens: suddenly. That's how everything happens. Her cataracts are so bad that her eyes look like eggs, the yolks slipping and sliding. "Oh," she said, "you brought *him*," refusing to remember Dad's name.

DAD: (yelling, as always) How are you, Alice?

GRANDMA: Where is she? (meaning Mom)

DAD: She'll be visiting soon.

GRANDMA: What's keeping her, then?

DAD: She has her hands full.

GRANDMA: Like hell.

DAD: Really, you can't imagine.

GRANDMA: She's a bitch, that's what! She never invites me over.

ME: Maybe she gets tired of you complaining about what a lousy housekeeper she is.

GRANDMA: The worst! And what a cook! Ugh. Want some Dinty Moore?

DAD AND I: We've eaten! (Nothing like canned stew to whet the appetite.)

Anyway, she turns on the TV—some game show where celebrities sit in squares and answer dumb questions like, "How did Borax get its name?" We watch with her for a while. Then, all of a sudden, her head drops to her chest. I look at Dad and he looks at me. We both know she's dead. Finally, he gets up and feels her pulse: "Narcolepsy," he says. We're both relieved as hell. We tiptoe out of there knowing that Grandma will be ticked off that we don't wake her so she can put her twenty or thirty dead bolts on.

*   *   *

In the car:

ME: Dad, what's gonna happen to Grandma when she gets too old to take care of herself?

DAD: Nursing home, I guess.

ME: Do you think Mom'll want her to move in with us?

DAD: Your mom's got too much to handle already.

ME: Bobby and I would help . . .

DAD: It just wouldn't work.

ME: All she ever does is watch TV. How could she be any trouble? Nursing homes are so horrible.

DAD: Yeah. They are. I mean, sad to say, but in some way, you hope that people die before it gets to that point. To be institutionalized like that . . .

(Dad looked like he was gonna cry, so I just changed the subject.)

ME: Dad, what did you want to be when you were young?

DAD: An inventor. I had a lot of ideas.

ME: Well, you *are* an inventor. You invent things all the time.

DAD: Yeah. But I never invent anything useful.

ME: Sure you do.

DAD: (smiling) Like what?

ME: Like that gadget that opens the window when

you pull the lever. (The thing broke after about three times.) That perfume warmer that goes on Mom's dressing table . . . I mean, the perfume really smells better warm. I really love the desk you made, Dad.

DAD: Well, you'll be in high school now. You'll probably have a lot more papers and stuff . . . notes from your boyfriends.

Dad smiles at me real big, and then we pull up to the house.

Anyway, it wasn't a bad day. For a few minutes, I even had a small feeling of newness.

September 10

High school. Cess pool. What more can I say? It's the same old thing only by a different name, with everybody hanging out in little groups. Within a week, it will be a grind. The school has this Scottish marching band. The guys parade around in skirts, their skinny legs stuck out of them like hairy golf clubs, carrying bagpipes. AND THEY PRACTICE ALL THE TIME. The big deal at this school is that they win a prize at the Rose Bowl parade every goddamn year and travel all over the world. I would consider joining, but only goody-two-shoes with wealthy parents (the uniforms and bagpipes cost a fortune) can.

It's raining. It's pounding. Maybe a flower or two will bloom. Then it'll dry up in the drought that's sure to follow. Here's the program. Fires, driven by the winds, burn up half the state each year. Then come the mud slides. To top it off, Mr. Meese assures us that our town is right smack on the San Andreas fault and we are fifty years overdue for a town-swallowing earthquake. Geology teachers love telling a bunch of pathetic adolescents this. It makes them feel powerful.

Astronomy class is pretty cool, though. I love studying the sky maps. We have great equipment, too. Some rich astronomer donated all kinds of stuff. When I showed Gloria (who hates science) a slide of Orion, she said it looked like menstrual blood on a Kotex. To Gloria, nothing is sacred.

I never mention the baby anymore to her. When I do, she pretends she's sticking her finger down her throat and is going to puke.

P.S. The stereotypes of high school gym teachers are true. Marine sergeants.

September 11

Coyotes were howling last night. A cat screamed, which will make it about the fifth cat who's been eaten this week. When Mom got all sentimental about the cats, I reminded her that we eat ground-up animals almost every night. "But they're not our pets!" she said.

"The cats are not the coyotes' pets either, Mom." I almost said "Einstein" instead of "Mom," but knew I'd get a slap. My parents aren't much for physical punishment, but I have gotten a well-deserved slap from Mom once in a while. If I were my own kid, I'd smack myself once a day. So, thank goodness I'm not.

Simon constantly grabs at me. He says he is conducting scientific experiments on the meaning of passion. Yesterday, he tried to put his hand up my shirt. Is this romance? I've heard of "great awakenings" in books and movies, of smoldering fires that ignite body and soul. I feel like the brunt of a huge joke; I'll never experience the adventure and excitement of romance. I just feel sorta grossed out.

September 12

My history teacher, Miss Faulkner, is a real dork.

She's from Alabama and has this accent that's as foreign as if she came from Russia. She went on and on about the "War of Northern Aggression." It took me about fifteen minutes to figure out that she was talking about the Civil War. She said the slaves were worse off after they were freed because they didn't get that good plantation food. This is *supposed* to be a course in *modern* history. Then she said she'll teach us some etiquette, since we are "terribly deprived" on account of living in heathen Southern California. She went on about salad forks and waiting until the host picks up his fork to pick up yours, and how to shake hands with someone who is missing an arm (!). What's *that* about?

I hate her.

Faulkner's one of those people who is so full of rules and regulations that there's no room for ideas.

My English teacher is cool, though. He said that school is a democracy and we should call him Sam. "Is that your name?" Gloria asked, like the smart-ass she is. "No," he answered with a straight face, "I said it's what you should *call me*." I guess he's a smart-ass, too. Also a hippie. He wears the same tie-dye T-shirt every day and has long hair. He said his first day there the principal came in with a big pair of scissors to cut off his ponytail, and that they agreed to play a game of poker to see if he got to keep it. Sam won.

I almost believe it. The principal's name is Mr. Franken; all that needs to be added is the "Stein" and he'd have a name that suits him.

Later: Couldn't sleep, so I watched a stupid movie about a civilization on Venus where the women run the planet and use men as sex slaves. Of course, the women fight over the foxiest man and can only make important political decisions if their manicures are finished and their hair is done. In the end, the men take over the planet, and order is restored. Ugh.

The myth of Venus as the planet of love is curious, since Venus is as hot as hell and surrounded by hurricane force winds. Of course this relates to the goddess for whom the planet is named. Poor Venus; her own love for Adonis resulted in her being killed by a wild boar. Ain't love grand.

September 13

I'm trying to figure out the mystery of Uranus, but math gets in the way. I never realized how dependent science is on math. It's a disappointment to my goal to be an astronomer, but I'll work it out somehow. How was Uranus knocked on its side? An asteroid? A spaceship? Because of its awkward position, each pole is subjected to forty-two years of constant sunlight or darkness, one after the other. If you were born on Uranus in one of the forty-two dark years you'd be 75 percent more likely to become an alcoholic, since all those dark places like Sweden have the highest alcoholism and suicide rates in the world. (Always knew Mom was from another planet.) Add to that the fact that Uranus has five moons, and you'd have one crazy population. This is my problem. I try to focus on the math and my mind does cartwheels through its own galaxy.

Bobby and Michelle joined the choir at the Unitarian church. Michelle started out as a Christian Scientist but had some falling-out with them over her parents' medical care. (They are both dead, so it can't have been very good.) Michelle reminds me of a pink mouse: pink dress, pink sweater with a little white lace collar. The two of them rehearse every night and stand there holding hands. It's pretty sickening, but I like her better now that I know she's a Unitarian.

*   *   *

September 15

Can't sleep. I thought of writing a letter to Simon, but I don't know what to say. The letter I would write is not the one he would like to receive. So I'll write to . . .

Dear Miss Faulkner: You are an idiot. Go back to the South where you came from and hire yourself a few slaves so you'll be happy. By the way, here are a few rules of etiquette you left off.

1. If teachers are idiots, ignore them.
2. If your mother's a drunk, don't tell the neighbors.
3. If an artist chops off a piece of his ear, pass it down to your descendants; it may be worth a fortune someday.
4. If you're going to fart in class, do it silently so no one knows it's you.
5. If a man *is* missing his arm, don't bother to shake his hand at all; he's probably too sad to care.

September 16

O'Neil says I'll be moved to honors classes next semester if I keep up the good work. I told him that I didn't want to do twice as much homework. He showed me the honors reading list: Homer, Virgil, Dante, Milton, Dostoyevsky, Kafka. I'll escape Miss Faulkner, but get to keep Sam.

Mom glanced at the honors permission slip, but she didn't really read it.

ME: Sign.

HER: You haven't done anything wrong?

ME: It's just a form to take some classes!

She signs, but still doesn't read it. Maybe it's silly but it makes me feel kind of disappointed, so I head out to the garage.

ME: Sign, Dad.

HIM: You didn't do something wrong?

(nice parents)

ME: (sigh)

HIM: (reading) Hey. Hey! Kristin. This is so groovy!

ME: Don't say "groovy," Dad. It makes you sound like you're about eighty.

DAD: You're going to be in honors classes!

ME: And the Eiffel Tower is in Paris.

HIM: I thought it was in Pisa. Ha!

What a dork.

Dad brought me a bunch of flowers. It was corn-ball, but kind of nice. The card said, "For my little scholar." Later, I started crying for no reason and couldn't stop myself until I finally fell asleep.

September 19

Bobby has become Mom's favorite. When I went downstairs, he was sitting at the table playing cards with her. She was gabbing about her childhood and how popular she was with boys and he was asking her questions about herself, just to be nice. "Wanna join our game, Kristin?" he asked.

"Nah," I said.

"She's too hoity-toity." Mom had to get her nasty two cents in.

God, I wish I lived somewhere else, someplace cold and wintery. Alaska? Sweden? I'd look for cracks in the ice and follow them deeper and deeper into the wild. I'd find the wolves and the coyotes and live with them.

September 20

Simon wants us to be each other's first sexual experiment. His rationale for this is that we don't have religious guilt about sex and that our minds match. He also thinks that we're good enough friends not to have this destroy our friendship. The whole idea is confusing, but I told him I'd think about it. As if I had said yes, he produced a Trojan rubber from his pocket—something I've seen in Bobby's room! If I'm gonna be a smoldering fire, I'll need someone with a little more finesse. But then again, it *would* be something. Sometimes I feel like pinching myself just to feel *something*. This is a dead-end town—no nature (with the exception of the mountains, which don't count since they're covered in smog); no rocks or sea, hardly any old houses; just mini-malls, fast-food restaurants, apartment buildings, condos, stucco, and smog.

September 21

It's so cool that Billie Jean King whipped Bobby Riggs at tennis. He's such a male chauvinist. Women are finally taking what they deserve. I called Simon to gloat, but he was at a seminar for "young artists." It's such a drag having a rich friend.

P.S. It's hard to decide who's grosser: Nixon or his V.P., Agnew.

September 23

Grandma has a cold. Why the hell do I bother to visit her? Last night, she raked Mom over the coals while she rubbed Vicks VapoRub over her chest. She coughed and sneezed her way down memory lane:

GRANDMA: There was an apartment in Detroit. This was before Detroit turned into the hellhole it is now. This was when people really loved and needed American cars. Then, Detroit was the place to be, I'm telling you, the place to be in the U.S.A. Morton and I'd walk around that city and say "American on wheels" to anyone who would listen. Isn't that hilarious? And Morton would pick flowers from my neighbor's window box and give them to me. He'd light me a cigarette from his cigarette like in that Bette Davis movie. We listened to the radio and danced. On our wedding night we were in a dance marathon; we were more interested in dancing than even going to bed, if you know what I mean. (long tragic pause) That was before your mother was born. Once your mother was born, Morton just wanted to go out by himself all the time.

Later: The ghost is howling like a coyote. Bobby wasn't home yet so I got into his bed. When I woke up, he was tiptoeing around.

BOBBY: It's okay. Go back to sleep. I'll sleep on the couch.

ME: What did you do tonight?

BOBBY: Just hung around Michelle's trailer. We were going to drive to the beach or something, but her aunt wanted her to stick around.

ME: What did you talk about?

BOBBY: I don't know. About what we're going to do when we graduate. About the church.

ME: Do you love Michelle?

BOBBY: Sure.

ME: Why?

BOBBY: It's easy to love Michelle. She's sweet and she's pretty. It's easy to love people in general.

ME: I think it's hard to love people. It's not that I don't want to. It's like I have . . . what's that thing when you have something in your eye that blocks your vision?

BOBBY: An astigmatism?

ME: Yeah, I have an astigmatism on my feelings.

BOBBY: Nah, you're just having a tough time these days. Do you want to watch TV?

ME: Okay. Bobby, do you love the ghost?

(He had to think about that for a while.)

BOBBY: I love him . . . because he's David. And . . . I hate him because he's not David. I can't help wondering what would have happened if I were just a few years older, if both of us . . . you know? (I shook my head.) David was the oldest and he always seemed smarter and bigger and better at everything than me. He got most of the attention, especially from Mom. But then, he had to go to war because he was the oldest . . . and that makes me feel, I don't know . . . guilty.

ME: I'm sorry, Bobby.

BOBBY: It's okay.

ME: Like the saying goes, "I didn't ask to be born."

BOBBY: Right.

ME: Or when.

September 24

I biked to the library, which is in the nice, older part of town. It's a good place to go when I need to escape. The librarian there, Miss Dodge, is pretty sweet; I've known her since I was about two. "Do you have something sophisticated for me to read?" I asked her, feeling dumb. She didn't grin at me like most adults do. "I just read a good piece in this magazine. It's on conspiracy theories surrounding Martin Luther King's assassination," she said. It was a pretty interesting article, but what got me really excited were the ads in the back of the magazine: L'École Gallavier.

SWISS BOARDING SCHOOL! The answer to all my problems. I copied down the address and, when I got home, wrote away for a brochure. I can't wait.

September 26

Something I've managed to avoid so far. I've been assigned to write a paper about the Vietnam War. It's bad enough that I have to listen to teachers going on and on about it as if there is nothing else that has ever happened in history.

September 27

Paper not started. If I don't write the thing I'll probably get an F, and down the drain with the honors program.

September 28

O'Neil was out sick, so I had to talk to Armstrong. "This is high school. We do our assignments. Really, history is not so bad," he says.

I can still read those damn books whether I'm in honors or not.

September 29

Brainstorming. Brain. Storming.

October 1

Notes for Vietnam paper:

<u>THE BAD WAR, by Kristin Folger</u>

There is no such thing as a good war, but some wars are worse than others. Such is the case with Vietnam.

Too stiff.

<u>FASCISM, by Kristin Folger</u>

The history of Vietnam is that many different forces have tried to govern it and the Vietnamese fought back. Ho Chi Minh was supposed to be a hero. But he wasn't. America got involved. President Kennedy tried to end the war, but then he was assassinated. Johnson made matters worse.

Too scattered.

October 2

<u>HOW IT STARTED, by Kristin Folger</u>

The French were wrong then Geneva was wrong Communism wrong capitalism wrong Vietcong wrong Eisenhower Kennedy Johnson Nixon you name it— the betrayed become the betrayers, the savior turns with a machine gun to the crowd.

* * *

This is how it happens: The young boy is taken from his home—he is bright, athletic, funny, a star. The town glories in his perfections: track star, wrestling star, star scholar.

But, he is still a child.

This is how it happens: The young boy is green as jade. He smiles, teeth bleached white from the sun, from Crest and Colgate and American dreams.

His country says war, says kill, says die, says don't question authority.

At first he doesn't mind. The uniform is shiny. Aren't American soldiers heroes? He's always thought they were. Inside, he pretends that he's someone else: John Wayne, Clark Gable. Outside, he excels, the way he always has. He trains to say war, say kill, say die. He flies to a land farther than he can imagine. He learns to be a soldier, to understand the terrain. He communes with nature. The snakes and lizards. The insects.

Part of him has gone away. The other part pretends he is in one of those movies he watched as a boy—*The Guns of Navarone, The Shores of Iwo Jima,* where the enemy is clear and ugly and evil. The enemy has a wicked face and a long skinny mustache. The enemy is not a woman farmer, a girl, a crying child, a scared teenager, a village.

This is the history of colonial rule. The changing of one land one body for another, one leg one arm one soul. And the whales travel miles to Baja, the turtles leave their eggs on the beach. And Simon, don't romanticize Ho Chi Minh or Marx or the maniac Stalin or Lenin or anyone or me. Don't even romanticize the whales, because they don't have difficult choices to make; they move on instinct. And the turtles leave their eggs on the beach to hatch alone. They don't even stick around to help their babies make it to the sea.

October 3

Dear Miss Faulkner: This is a late paper. After you read it, you may understand why. I can't write about the American participation in the Vietnam War without thinking of my brother David. Before he went to war, he was pretty famous at this school. He was a track star, wrestling champ, valedictorian. David was going to be a doctor or an astronomer.

Did I tell you that David knew the name of every planet, every constellation? We walked a lot at night and he introduced me to the stars. He taught me to see the way light falls on the trees, how to observe the changing directions of the wind, how to know when the rain would come days before it came. We talked about God. He believed in God, but he said it was okay if I didn't. He wanted people to think that things came easy for him. But they didn't. He would stay up nights working on his wrestling moves or his Spanish or his debate speech. David made birthday cakes in the shapes of animals. David sang old Gershwin songs off-key. Forget it, Miss Faulkner. You wouldn't understand. You think the slaves should have stayed enslaved.

October 4

I'm going to fail history. Naturally, I didn't give

the paper or letter to Miss Faulkner. Why bother writing to even you? Why pretend that you're somebody and you can hear me?

Later: Called St. Agnes and a nun gave me the number of a convent in Alta Dena. The Mother Superior was eager enough to talk to a potential novice (if that's what it's called). She got right on when I explained my interest. The nun business has been slow lately, I'm sure. All that poverty and celibacy; there must not be many takers in this country. Also, that marriage to Christ business is pretty weird. In every religion there's always something that rubs me the wrong way. She asked if I'd been confirmed and I told her I had. (That was an event in itself—Mom dressed me up like a Chatty Cathy doll, complete with patent leather shoes!) The Mother Superior explained that I could come to the convent to live at any time, but that my parents would have to give permission, plus pay room and board until I become a real nun. I was pretty cheerful, imagining myself holed up in a nice stark room somewhere reading Descartes and Heidegger, until she went over the daily routine: three Masses a day for an hour each, cooking, cleaning, milking cows (!). When I asked if I'd have to attend Mass since I'm an atheist, she immediately lost interest. What's the problem?

October 5

David. Please. Please come back. Please. Even with your body screwed up you could still do things. You could be a doctor even, like you wanted to. We could live together forever, and I'd help you out. Please, Dave. You've rested enough. Come back.

October 15

I dreamt about David. It was like he was here, in the room with me, and it was the past. Usually dreams come in pieces, like someone took a reel of film and cut it up, but this was a whole. "What do you think about those astronauts?" he said.

"Which ones?" I asked.

"The ones who are going to the moon."

"I'd hate to be in a little capsule. Eating all that weird freeze-dried food," I said.

"Oh, it would be worth it. To be able to investigate space, to make discoveries."

"That would be cool."

"Yep. Cool." He turned, as if to go.

"I'll go into space, if you will!"

"It's good to see you, little sister."

"Don't go!"

"The lieutenant says I'm up next for leave. I'll be home in no time."

"Pleeease," I begged.

"I'll be back," he said. Then he disappeared.

October 16

Dear David:

Come back, like you promised in the dream. Come back with your blond hair, your white smile, your tanned face that already had smile lines.

Every thing I do is in your memory. I'm working hard at school, like you did.

The atoms that make up the earth are formed inside of stars. In that sense, you could say that all of life begins with a star.

October 18

Bobby talked me into joining the choir at the Unitarian church. He says it'll help prepare our voices for our brother/sister act (which is obviously never going to amount to anything). Only dorks sing in choirs, but at least it'll get me out once in a while.

*   *   *

P.S. Now that Agnew has resigned, what will happen to Nixon? I can't tell you how good it is to see them caught in their trap. It's not even Watergate that was so bad, but the war. The war. When will this whole thing be over?

October 19

Saved by O'Neil. O'Neil had a discussion with Miss Faulkner. Since I never turned in my Vietnam paper, I will be able to write about World War II and get my grade changed to a B. O'Neil's pretty nice, even if he is a geek. He makes me feel a little nervous though, like someone's riding a bike in my stomach, and they don't know how to put on the brakes.

October 20

Some snapshots from my day:

1. Wake up to a list of chores. My reward will be dinner out—Chinese.

2. A bunch of boring stuff.

3. Afternoon—Carol comes over in hysterics because Freddie has disappeared and supposedly dropped her. Carol gets so sobby that she wipes her nose on whatever suits her, includ-

ing my beaded sweater, the one piece of clothing I actually like. When I tell her not to snot on my sweater, she says "Sorry," but she really means "You insensitive bitch." Which is true. I couldn't care less about Freddie.

4. Freddie shows up, with a sprained ankle: "Look at these bitchin' crutches," he shouts. They are so excited at seeing each other that their tongues meet in space, like two magnets. They don't even say good-bye as they move, glued together, out the door. Dad says, "Nice to see you, too."

5. Finally get to the Chinese restaurant. Grateful to be removed from Mom's tasteless slop for one night. There is an hour-and-a-half wait.

6. We get seated. Mom and Dad are in a peachy mood due to the fact that they have sipped mai tais in the bar. They act like Carol and Freddie and ignore me.

7. Mom insists on ordering chow mein, egg fu yung, egg rolls, and moo goo gai pan. Everything she can think of that has no flavor.

8. The food tastes like Mom's tasteless slop, only with the charming addition of cornstarch and soy sauce.

9. Fortune cookies:

Mom's—Your wisdom is a treasure for all who surround you.

Dad's—When you walk the people cherish your footsteps.

Mine—If the world is a lamp of doom you must use elbow grease to make it shine.

Now what the hell is that supposed to mean?

October 21

I wish O'Neil had chosen something less depressing.

Six million Jews and "undesirables" (gypsies, homo-sexuals, cripples, midgets, the mentally ill) were mur-dered (exterminated) during World War II. The pictures of the faces in the library book look like mine: dark, broad, heavy eyebrows, frizzy hair. I asked my mother if we have any Jewish blood in our family. "Yeah, my grandmother was Jewish."

Surprise! "On whose side?"

"Grandma's—my mom's mom. I think that's why she's so cheap."

I can't believe it. All these years of being dragged to the Catholic church when I'm really a Jew through the maternal line. Amazing! And there's my mom—the anti-Semite. "That's why she's so cheap . . ."

ME: That means we're Jews, Mom.

MOM: It means no such thing. I was born and raised a Catholic. My dad was a Catholic.

ME: Morton? The family deserter?

MOM: Don't start in on my dad. He wrote me a real nice letter one time, explaining everything. He said that he just couldn't take living with my mom anymore but that he still loved me. And he promised to visit real soon and bring me some pretty things.

ME: Did he?

MOM: Well, no. But we moved so often . . . he probably couldn't track us down. We didn't have any stability!

ME: I think I'd like to visit a concentration camp. Would you take me to Auschwitz?

MOM: You *would* ask to go to Auschwitz for a vacation.

ME: An educational trip, that's all.

MOM: (laughing) Ask your father, Moneybags, for a ticket to Europe! I'm sure he can pull it right out of his pockets.

*   *   *

On the gates of Auschwitz it said, "Work Will Set You Free."

October 22

Attempting to reduce, Mom takes walks around the block every afternoon. It's no accident that this coincides with my coming home from school. Everything I do seems to get on her nerves. While she's out, I sneak into her room, get the key, and go visit the ghost. He's a pretty scary sight. He's lost so much weight that he looks like a skeleton in clothes. One side of his body is fine; the other side is mangled, his leg severed below the knee, the arm useless.

I look for a trace, a sliver, a speck of what used to be David. If I can find it, then it'll be okay. A trace of shine, a sliver of glass, a speck of stardust. I talk to him. If he's drugged, he moans, just stares like Grandma does. If the drugs are wearing off, he can get pretty violent.

David, you must be in there somewhere.

October 23

Bobby and Michelle dragged me to *The Way We Were*, with Barbra Streisand and Robert Redford. It was pretty cornball, but I had to admire the Streisand character, who was a social activist. Plus, Redford is pretty good-looking, although his acting consists of clenching and unclenching his jaw.

Simon hasn't been at church. I called and asked where's he's been. "Love is painful, Kristin," he said. "I can't look and not touch. I have too much passion for that." Creepy! Creep.

Singing with the church choir isn't so bad. The "conductor" is this spacey guy with long blond hair and a leather fringed vest, who flirts with all the girls. If he even tries with me, I'll punch him in the mouth. His name is Eric Aldo. When we sing, he closes his eyes and sways like an evangelist. Some of the songs are hokey. When Michelle sang "I Don't Know How to Love Him," from *Jesus Christ Superstar*, I thought she would float away in her own sweetness. But the singing gets me out of myself. I think it's what the existentialists call engagé. Bobby has become Aldo's "right-hand man" (meaning he has to stay behind and fold up the chairs), so Michelle took me out for an ice cream. She's an only child, so she gets a kick out of playing big sister. The only problem is that she acts like I'm eight instead of two years younger than her. Oh well. She's okay. I try to be nice to her because she is a total goody-two-shoes. Her mother died when she was nine and her dad died last year. Now she lives with her aunt in a trailer park, and Bobby says it's real run-down and depressing. The aunt insists on putting on airs and keeps antiques in the trailer instead of selling them so they can eat. I can see why Michelle is in such hog heaven with Bobby. Bobby is loyal and treats her like she's a princess. Which reminds me: Bobby says he is planning to go to DENTAL SCHOOL! Can you believe it? Talk about sick. Bobby says the whole issue is money.

"Why would you want to have people breathing their stomach contents in your face all day?" I ask. He doesn't want to scrape and worry about money the way Mom and Dad do. He doesn't want his wife (meaning Michelle?) to lose her sense of beauty in life worrying about whether the electricity will be shut off.

Bobby remembers a time when Mom was happy and smiley and always wanting to do something fun. The combination of David and being broke has changed her.

It makes me sad to think of Mom like that, and of

her just being sour all the time now. It would be a tragedy if she became one of those women in curlers who stands in the doorway and makes lewd comments to the paperboy.

October 24

Body changes again. A giant betrayal! I need a larger bra. My hips have spread apart like two wishbones being pulled from either side. I'm still bony though. You could serve soup from the concave spaces.

Later: When I went in to see the ghost, he was on the floor. As much as I tried to help him up, I couldn't. I knelt beside him. It seemed like he was trying to say something to me, but it all came out garbled. Suddenly, his fist came up hard, right into my jaw. God, it hurt! I fell backwards. His eyes were scary since he was so angry, and I was afraid that if I got into his grip, he might strangle me. I stood up and backed out of the room. I locked the door. When Mom came home I said, "You'd better check on the ghost . . . he's squawking up a storm."

October 26

Hurrah! My Swiss boarding school brochure finally came. It looks fabulous. Girls come from all over the world to study. In addition to the usual subjects, there is French, Latin, Greek, archery, ballet, art appreciation, and equestrian activities (meaning horseback riding). The school is at a renovated château of some kind and is gorgeous, with fountains and gardens. The letter is from a Mademoiselle Fontaine, and she "wishes my gracious presence there more than she can express." It's twenty thousand dollars a year, but I probably eat at least half of that here. I've just got to go! I can't wait until Mom gets home from her walk.

Later: I am about as ticked off as I've ever been. Without even looking at the brochure, Mom just laughed in her nasty way. "Twenty thousand dollars!" she laughed, as if it was the funniest thing in the world.

"Don't you care about my education?" I said.

"Not twenty thousand dollars' worth." Then to be polite she added, "Besides, I'd miss you too much."

There's a literary term from English vocab that describes Mom to a T: "anticlimactic." That's Mom. The anticlimax to anything exciting or interesting.

I'll wait for Dad to come home and ask him.

∗   ∗   ∗

Later: Dad's reply to my European education scheme was just as bad as Mom's, although he put things more kindly. "Really, Kristin, if I could afford to send you to Switzerland, I would. I can barely keep a roof over our heads."

"Who cares about a roof, if your mind isn't free?"

"It doesn't take twenty thousand dollars a year to free your mind. All you have to do is go to the library."

"You don't understand, Dad. This is about my future."

"Don't you think we all want something we can't have?"

October 27

Carol and Freddie came over last night.

Freddie made a big deal out of climbing the stairs on his hands. How could somebody who is so brain-fried have such good balance? It must be a savant thing.

They sat on my bed and managed to talk without their tongues in each other's mouths.

THE CONSPIRATORS: We're worried about you.

ME: Me? Why?

THE CONSPIRATORS: You don't seem to have fun anymore. We think that maybe you're in a funk.

ME: Your idea of fun is listening to Black Sabbath records and giggling about the dust on the carpet.

FRED: It totally looks like the Sahara down there.

ME: You have such an interesting way to travel.

CAROL: I mean, you won't even go out with Simon. And he has a major crush on you.

ME: Simon doesn't want to go out with me.

FRED: We think we should fix you up . . .

ME: Who with?

CAROL: You don't need to sound so haughty.

FRED: Mason.

ME: Mason?!

CAROL: He's real cute.

ME: Give me a break.

CAROL: At least come to a party or something.

ME: I told you . . . I have better things to do with my time!

FRED: Mason is going to be a motocross star, man. He can ride his bike up a ramp, rotate five times in the air before coming down. Or I could introduce you to my older brother, Frank. He's coming back from clown school in France. He flunked out, but still, he can juggle seven eggs at a time without breaking any.

ME: Clown school in France?

FRED: So you'll go with him.

ME: No. But I must admit that's interesting.
FRED: I'll tell him to call you.
CAROL: Freddie!
FRED: Oh, it's no big deal.
CAROL: He likes boys!
FRED: He'll change.

After I told them to go home, I felt really bummed out. Carol and I bought our first Barbies and rode our first bikes together. I caught chicken pox from her. She caught strep throat from me.

Now, there's a canyon between me and everybody else. And all I can do is fall into the space between.

Later: Carol and Freddie move fast.

A "date" showed up for me at 6:00 tonight. A boy whose face seemed vaguely familiar. He brought flowers and wore a suit and tie. There I was in my T-shirt and jeans, shocked to pieces. "A boy has come to take you on a date," my mother whispered. She rarely talks to me, so I thought it was a joke.

"What date is that?"

"You know. Your date. The one you were telling me about."

I started to say that I never told her about a date, but she disappeared. I burst into the kitchen all ready to tell this guy where to go. But what could I do? There he stood, clutching a handful of yellow roses, looking totally nervous. "I hope Freddie told you what time I'd be here . . ."

"Yes. Right." I figured we were going to the prom, the way he was dressed. "Where are we going?"

"The Way We Were."

"Seen it."

"It's very romantic."

I shoved the flowers in a vase, which fell over. Great. Anyway, I saw *The Way We Were* yet again. This time I was annoyed with *both* Streisand and Redford. Because he seemed to know me so well, I never asked the boy's name and still don't know it. I felt bad telling him that I wouldn't go out with him again. "It's not you," I said, as nicely as possible. "I'm just not in the mood to see anyone."

"Do you like model cars?" he asked, as if he hadn't heard me.

"Not really."

"'Cause I have a real cool collection and they're hanging from the ceiling in my room. My mom hangs them on invisible wire. Well, it's uh, not like I couldn't hang them myself. She just does it 'cause I'm busy. Want to come over and look at them?"

"No thanks." I slammed the door, and now I'm spending the whole evening feeling guilty about traumatizing an adolescent boy.

October 28

Guess what? Another date showed up tonight! It never occurred to me that they would send another! This one I knew. Matt—a kid who almost died in seventh grade when he fell off the bleachers. He took me to a small airport in the desert, where we looked at his father's planes. He gave me a canned daiquiri that he found in the cockpit. It tasted like bad lemonade. Then he said, "Mind if I kiss you with a sore throat and cold?"

"Nah." What the hell else could I say? "Maybe I'll get lucky and it'll kill me!"

"Huh?"

"The sore throat and cold. Just . . . let me finish my drink first. That'll make it more palatable."

"Whoa."

"What?"

"Freddie and Carol said you were a trip and you are. You are a trip."

"A trip to Vegas or a trip to China?"

"Oh, heh heh. You're definitely Vegas. A Vegas showgirl!"

After I recovered from having his tongue abuse my tonsils, I asked him to take me home.

"But why?" he whined.

"You didn't give the right answer. I am . . . a trip to China."

"Shit," he said. "I never win anything."

October 30

Much to my surprise, Vera Thompson invited me to her Halloween party. She's pretty weird and behind the times—she thinks that David Cassidy and Bobby Sherman are still popular—but since she's the only one having a party, just about everyone is going. It will do me good to get out of the house.

October 31

I dressed as a gypsy tonight. Found an old red dress of Mom's, and tied scarves all around myself. I put a ton of makeup on. It was fun. Before the party, I stopped by Grandma's. It was nice to see her in a good mood. It seems she's had a companion lately, a man named Italo she met at the senior citizens' potluck. She was so excited about my costume and went on about how I should be a model. Grandma's pretty slim on compliments, so I was flattered. I noticed that she had a couple of bottles of wine in the house. She said that Italo loves wine and then she offered me a glass.

GRANDMA: Kristin, guess what?

ME: What, Grandma?

GRANDMA: (giggling) We did it.

ME: (dense as hell) What?

GRANDMA: Me and Italo. We did it. We're doing it . . . regularly.

For a second, I swear, I thought she was talking about bowel movements, one of her favorite subjects.

ME: Grandma! Do you mean sex?

GRANDMA: And in ways I never thought of! Under the kitchen table; oh, that was a little hard on my back. With the TV off. In time with music. In the backseat of his car. In the elevator!

ME: In the elevator?!

GRANDMA: Oh, don't you worry. We stopped it between floors. In fact, that was Italo's job, before he retired, inspecting elevators. He knows everything about them.

ME: (Do I need to hear this?) Well, I better go now.

GRANDMA: Do you know how many years it's been?

ME: Uh, no.

GRANDMA: Thirty. Can you believe it? It was never fun with Morton. If I'd known it could be fun I'd have done it sooner.

ME: Oh, well, that's something.

GRANDMA: I was lonely, Kristin. I tried to pretend that my shows and my apartment were enough, but it's not true.

ME: That's . . . good. (What else could I say?) Thanks for the wine, Grandma.

GRANDMA: Don't tell your mother, alright? Don't tell her . . . anything. She never approves of anything I do. Whew. Wonders never cease.

The party was okay. Some people were high, which I can't get into. It's not that I'm a goody-two-shoes; I just don't like being out of it; I don't think it feels good and it reminds me of the ghost. Gloria was at the party. She's making a documentary about homeless people in Los Angeles. I didn't know there were any. Carol and Freddie were nowhere to be seen, which was good, because I'm really mad at them. And of course Simon, decked out like a robot, cornered me.

SIMON: Did I tell you I'm in love with you?

ME: Not lately.

SIMON: You think I'm kidding, don't you? I'm not. I love you.

ME: Everyone knows that gypsies and robots don't fall in love.

SIMON: It's no joke. I want to do something about it.

ME: Get over it.

He looked crushed, so I said, "Simon, I really miss your friendship. . . . Please stop being in love with me so we can be friends."

"If you let me kiss you, I'll be cured."

As much as I hated the idea, I went outside with him. He kissed me and, maybe it was the wine, but it was kind of fun.

SIMON: I'm not cured.

ME: If we could just be friends, Simon, then . . .

I started crying, which was totally embarrassing. He looked all worried and ran around to find Kleenex. Since hormones have kicked in, I will cry at any time, which is truly disgusting.

I'd like to sleep now, but I can hear Mom and Dad arguing in the kitchen. Hardly a soothing sound.

*   *   *

November 2

The ghost is sick. A doctor from the VA hospital came to see him and gave him antibiotics.

Later: I snuck into the ghost's room. It was strange. Instead of being his usual violent self, he was stretched out on his bed, still as a rock. I thought he was dead, and for a second, I was relieved. It was only when I got closer that I saw the heavy blanket rising and falling against his chest. His eyes were open and the rims were red, like targets around the blue of his eyes. "David," I whispered. "I know you're in there." The ghost looked back at me, his eyes rolling up. He seemed so sick, so miserable, that I felt sorry for him. Even though I hate him for taking my brother's place.

November 5

Last week, I was walking up Glendora Mountain Road. I came right up to a coyote. Coyotes are scavengers. They move in packs, like elephants. Not many people know this, but coyotes are one of the smartest animals that exist. No one can trap a coyote because it's capable of deciphering and outsmarting a trap. For some reason, she was alone. We stared at each other. Her tan fur made her almost indistinguishable from the mountainside. I felt very close to her. She cocked her head like she was trying to understand something. This went on for a minute, then I heard a howl from far away. Someone was calling her. Almost in unison, we turned and went our separate ways.

Why can't I ever feel that way with people? I want to. So much. I want to feel on a level with someone so that we'll know each other deeply, without even talking. It's not even reading thoughts. Because thoughts contain language. And language gets in the way. It's more . . . a oneness or something. I can't explain. I know I sound romantic. So I'll stop.

November 7

Dreamt about the coyote, that we were walking on the beach together. The sand was the color of her fur, of my skin. Jellyfish, crabs like little pearly spiders moved around us on spindly legs.

The sound of the universe is a hum. I hear it when I'm in nature. David said the sound is ohm. The sound of ohm is an affirmation.

Sometimes, even the dead grass and the hazy poisonous sunsets, the freeway, the trees, the earth, the painted houses with their carefully placed gardens, seem part of this hum—and I am part of this hum and it is called life everlasting because even if the entire animal and plant kingdoms are annihilated by atom bombs, meteorites, or the collapse of the sun—even so, the sound will continue and somewhere a cockroach will start things up again and the hum will grow louder and louder and louder again.

November 9

Even though it's happened every month, I can't get used to it! Started my goddamned period, yet again. I just love feeling poetically suicidal once a month. Still, I do get out of gym class. Hopefully Mrs. Bodger won't remember that I had my period just a week ago. I mean, this is the real thing after all.

Later: Looking in the mirror is shocking. I don't recognize my face at all. I no longer recognize my body. How can I describe it? That my body is a desert with sand everywhere; gold, tan, beige, and white. There are caves in some places and strangers live there. Without paying rent.

November 12

Woke up at 3:00 this morning. I went to the

kitchen, and there was Mom. She's started smoking again and from the looks of the ashtray, she'd been at it all night.

"Kristin, your father and I are getting a divorce. Who're you gonna live with?"

Bam! Just like that. I didn't know what to say. I felt like someone had tied a scarf around my neck and was pulling it from either side. Like I was going to be sick. All these years they've fought, but I thought at the bottom they cared about each other.

November 13

Bobby took me to Bob's Big Boy for hot fudge cake. We racked our brains about how to get Mom and Dad to stop acting like babies. "They're not meant to divorce," Bobby kept saying, as if he had some in with the Fates. He's even more upset than I am. Now, I just feel numb. "How could this happen?" he asked me.

"I don't know," I said.

We sat there for about two hours and came up with some pathetic ideas to keep them together, like pretending Dad has a girlfriend to make Mom jealous. I even created a name, Iris: Iris, the bowling alley cocktail waitress who wears too much perfume and chain-smokes. She's not very classy, of course, but she's a heck of a lot of fun.

November 15

Cornered Dad and asked him why he's willing to destroy our family at the drop of a hat. "It's more than a hat that's dropped, Kristin," he said sadly. "It's just a trial separation. Just a trial. It's what your mother wants."

November 17

Bobby had a long talk with Mom last night. I wanted to be a part of the conversation, but he said no because I "incite" her (whatever that's supposed to mean). I did listen in from the hall. It was pretty lame, with Bobby mumbling, "Didn't you marry Dad for *better* or *worse?*"

"Not this worse," she said.

Iris the cocktail waitress would never let a good man like Dad get away. She would wear a feather boa and fishnet stockings and play Frank Sinatra records instead of just whining all the time.

Why can't changes ever be good?

∗   ∗   ∗

November 19

Went to see David to tell him about Mom and Dad's divorce. If the real David were here, he would solve everything. Of course, the ghost only stared at me. Still sick. A thin thread of saliva running from his mouth. I couldn't look at him.

Who will look after the ghost? Mom or Dad?

November 21

Saw Mr. Causeway at Woolworth's. I ducked behind the laundry baskets in housewares, but he spotted me.

CAUSEWAY: How's it going, Kristin?

ME: Okay.

CAUSEWAY: Planning on doing the laundry, or just avoiding me?

ME: My mom always has me do the laundry. She's kind of crazy, you know.

CAUSEWAY: You don't say.

ME: Yep.

CAUSEWAY: I've been in the hospital again. Gallstones. The size of golf balls.

ME: I'm sorry.

CAUSEWAY: Too much meat.

ME: Oh.

CAUSEWAY: I don't eat meat anymore. You know, they put all kinds of things in meat. It's not just meat. There's hormones and chemicals. But the gallstones are gone, so I'm okay. Back to Robert Frost, Yeats, all those guys who give life meaning.

ME: Right. (It's just like Causeway to think that the only poets are "guys"!)

CAUSEWAY: How's everything going in high school?

ME: Great. I'm getting straight A's.

CAUSEWAY: So I heard. I was at Mr. O'Neil's wedding last weekend and he said you were doing well.

ME: O'Neil's . . . wedding?

CAUSEWAY: It was a nice affair.

ME: I didn't know he was getting married.

CAUSEWAY: Lovely girl, his wife. Petite. Dark-haired, like you. Well, I'm glad high school agrees with you, Kristin.

O'Neil married! It kinda makes me sick.

You'd think he would've told me or something. What a traitor, becoming a member of the bourgeoisie like that.

Later: Talking to Causeway bugged me for some reason; it's like I was in a battle only to discover that the enemy was related to me. I don't do the kind of pranks I did on him anymore. I'm now merely deflated like in the French movie with the red balloon, only no bouquet of balloons has appeared to carry me over the rooftops of Paris.

December 1

Thanksgiving was about as depressing as it gets. Grandma went out with Italo. Mom bought Swanson's frozen turkey and stuffing dinners, which we ate in front of the TV. We watched the stupid parade, then *The Wizard of Oz*. The whole time, Dad was putting his things in boxes. No one said a blessing this year, because none of us was feeling very thankful, not even to the Pilgrims who came to these shores only to infect the Indians with their diseases and slaughter them.

I wish a tornado would come along and sweep us into Oz. You can bet that when it came time to click my heels together, I wouldn't bother to say, "There's no place like home."

P.S. Mom said that Swanson makes a better turkey than her. Sadly true.

December 3

Introduced the concept of Iris to Mother.
ME: What do you think of that woman Dad's seeing?

MOM: Your dad is seeing someone?

ME: Her name is Iris. She's got blond hair and wears sexy clothes and fishnet stockings.

Much to my horror, Mom started laughing hysterically.

MOM: That's a joke! Right? Your dad on a date! The only romantic feelings he has are for his power saw.

December 15

Dad has moved into a furnished apartment. Stucco exterior, brown doors in a line. Inside, the predictable fake wooden coffee table (for a man who loves well-made furniture), green shag carpet, and tweed foldout couch. The center of the apartment is, what else, the television. What American could live without one? It's a studio apartment, so we just sit on the foldout couch and watch *Wild Kingdom* and the news. It all feels so weird. I don't know what to say. Bobby stayed with Dad a few nights until I begged him not to. "Please, Bobby," I said, "It's too creepy without you here."

"It's creepy at Dad's, too," he said. "There's no place to move around. This whole thing is wrong."

December 16

Mom and Dad have gone over their new arrangements. They can't sell the house, since it's been refinanced past its actual value . . . God knows how they managed that.

Pathetic. Mom drinks vodka and orange juice and goes through the paper every night with a red marker, circling jobs. When she asks my opinion I say, "How 'bout being a bartender?"

"I was so happy when I found out you were a girl. I pictured the mother-daughter outings, shopping for clothes, dressing you in ruffles." She takes a long swig. "But you would only wear jeans and boys' shirts. You had every dress torn to smithereens, or filthy in no time."

Mom has always been pretty, well dressed. Lately, she wears the same orange shirt with the wheelbarrow buttons and dirty slacks. "Sounds like I'm a pretty big disappointment," I say.

"You're you, that's all. I wish I'd have had your *chutzpa*. You'll do fine in life."

"So today, you get to be Jewish."

She waves at me. I'm dismissed. Then (like she does every night), she crumples up the newspaper, and throws it in the trash.

December 20

God, what a mess in the kitchen: overturned coffee cups, grounds spread on the counter, empty packages, soda cans, rotting oranges in a plastic bowl. The white curtains are filthy and pulled to the side with safety pins. The windowsill is covered with dust and what looks like congealed honey; something sticky anyway. Since this divorce business, Mom has become a major slob.

I poured bleach over every surface. Stood on one of the torn vinyl chairs and tugged the curtains off their frames. Outside, it might as well be summer. The kids across the street were slamming themselves on a Slip 'N Slide. The arc of the sprinkler made the water silver because the sun was that hot. The kids' legs were so white. In summer, they'd be beet red. Three years ago, I'd have dashed across the street and flung myself down that slippery wet path in my clothes. I'd have planned races and games for everyone, and come home with sprinkler cuts on my ankles and toes, my skin shriveled from the water like an old lady's.

Then Mom came in: "What is that smell?"

"It's bleach. I'm cleaning the kitchen."

"Well, it's about time, isn't it?"

You're welcome!

January 5, 1974

Two weeks of boring vacation. Forgive me for

being away so long. Something about the holiday season left me speechless. Christmas is a weird holiday anyway, the way Americans turn it into one giant shopping spree.

When we were little, it was fun. The three of us kids would rush downstairs and put the presents into piles. We'd make breakfast for Mom and Dad, usually burnt French toast or something, then David and Dad would put together all the bicycles and stuff that needed to be constructed.

This Christmas was depressing. Bobby and I spent part of the day with Mom, part of it with Dad. Dad bought me a nice leather jacket. Grandma came over to our house and gave Mom a toaster. I made a long braided key chain for David out of leather, as if he will ever have keys.

On New Year's Eve, Dad actually came over and brought Mom a bottle of champagne. Grudgingly, she drank it with him. Mom's New Year's resolution was to "reduce" and find "a decent job" (should be to stop drinking). Dad's was to finish the cabinet he's building (should be to talk to Mom when he comes over, rather than stare off into space). Bobby and I went to his room, to allow them to be alone. Our resolution—to get Mom and Dad back together. Later, Michelle came over and we played Masterpiece (my Christmas present from Bobby). It's a pretty cool game with famous paintings that you auction off; maybe I'll be an art historian when I grow up.

January 10

Never thought I'd say this, but it's a relief to be back at school. The honors program is work-intensive and despite the irony of the Auschwitz gates, work does make me free. I've got about a million reports to write. In my report on *Beowulf* I explain why Grendel and his mother are the only civilized characters (because his mother loves him so much). That should go over like a lead balloon. I probably should've stuck with my safe bet, the transition from paganism to Christianity. The teacher went over that for three classes. It's a cool book. The part where Beowulf dies had me crying my eyes out.

I'm in class with nerds now. All the eggheads are with me: the scrawny undeveloped dorks, the shy, the antisocial, the kids I've gone to school with for years, but have never spoken to. I remember these faces from grade school. They were among the last to be chosen for teams, just like me.

* * *

Really, it's not so bad. They speak quickly, smartly, like even their voices are wearing glasses, rather than in the slurred pothead drawl of kids like Carol, Vera, and Freddie. And some of their brains are refreshing. There's something to be said for being unpopular, I guess. It allows kids time to get smart.

Simon has a mustache. It's a fuzzy line over the top of his mouth, like Hitler's, a shade darker than peach. He feels this increases his virility. He spent all of history class stroking it. I asked him if we could get together. "I'll try to transcend my feelings," he said. "I'll take a cold shower and come by tomorrow." Give me a break!

January 11
I went to see *The Exorcist* with Bobby. It was gross. In one scene this girl's head spins around her neck and she throws up guacamole. I almost puked myself.

January 12
David's birthday came and went without celebration or discussion.

"Couldn't we make the ghost a cake, or something?" I asked Mom.

"I told you not to call him that!" she said. "Now go to your room!" And that was it.

How long can this keep up? To pretend that he doesn't exist, when he's there all the time. To pretend. And Mom watches *The Waltons* and says, "What a nice family."

"They're actors, Mom. John-Boy probably cheats on his wife and takes acid."

"He does no such thing! Go to your room!"

It's getting to be her refrain.

January 14

A specialist was by to see David and he was taken to the hospital. Dad came over to the house and spoke in a low voice to Bobby, while Mom paced the kitchen asking the doctor questions. When I came down, though, Dad told me to stay out of Mom's way, to "lessen the confusion," but I watched out the window as the ambulance came. The ghost was strapped to a stretcher and carted off.

The war.

*   *   *

January 15

Mom is like a zombie. She's so worried about David. Nobody will tell me anything. I feel like I'm going to explode. When I asked Dad if he could take me to the hospital, he said, "If he was really in that bad shape, I'd take you. But the VA hospital is not a pretty place. The smell alone will make you retch."

January 16

Mom is so upset that she actually invited Grandma over. For once, Grandma didn't make snide remarks about Mom's housekeeping. They both drank vodka and watched TV, then Grandma and I went up to David's room and dusted and aired it. While we were wiping David's trophies off, Grandma started crying, remembering the times he won them. I was crying, too, but I kept my back turned so she wouldn't know. "That's better," Grandma said when the room was clean. "I feel like I have to do something in these situations."

January 20

Had a discussion with Simon about life after death. He believes in reincarnation. He feels that people should be buried with as many possessions as possible in order to maintain a memory of the present life in the next one, like the Egyptian princes. One minute he's an atheist—the next, this. To make matters worse, he broke his promise and digressed into sex. He says that the Romans threw up after every meal and had sex with each other all the time even if they were related; to this, he attributes the brilliance of their empire. Everyone knows this was their downfall.

People are a disappointment. David not improving. Bobby busy with Michelle. Simon still lurching at me. Carol in love with Freddie. The ol' parents wrapped up in their own dramas. Despite their separation, they've continued with the therapy, which is a mistake. Average people do not respond well to introspection.

Later: Midnight. Just woke up with this thought: Maybe Simon's right. Maybe there *is* a spirit that ejects from the body. Even stars, when they die, eject hydrogen and helium from their bodies, which fly out in space into infinity.

January 21

The doctor says that David's kidneys are damaged, but he is responding well to medication. They suggested, though, that he be entered as an inpatient at the VA hospital's psychiatric ward. "You won't let them do it, will you, Mom?" I asked.

She didn't answer.

January 24

The ghost is back from the hospital.

What is it the Buddhists say? That desire is the cause of misery. I guess I hoped that he'd be better mentally, too.

I brought out my record player and played the Beach Boys and the Beatles real loud, all of the music he used to love.

The ghost is here, but no sign of my David.

January 25

Eric Aldo took me aside and asked me to stop calling him Mister Aldo; he feels it elevates him above me. "I don't want to be elevated in any way, shape, or form. The Unitarian church is a place where everyone is equal and everyone is invited; all races, religions, even gays," he said. While he talks, he sways so that his words seem very important and holy. Then he said, "Besides,

Kristin, the way you say 'Mister' is the way most people would say 'Screw you.'" My jaw must've dropped about a foot. But then I thought about it and I realized that when I trust someone, I usually call them by their first or last name, like O'Neil. I never call him Mister. So the rest of the night, I said his name real sweetly, "Errric," the way the rest of the girls do—about forty times 'til he looked like he was gonna lose it.

Afterwards Bobby asked, "What did Eric say to you?"

I told him.

"Good," he said. "I thought he might hit on you. He's hit on about ten girls already. It's pretty bad."

January 27

I need to stay out of Mom's hair, so I've joined the drama club. It's where all the weirdos hang out, so I should fit right in. The first day the teacher, Miss Briar, had us mirror each other. This kid, Roman, kept his tongue stuck out the entire time and I had to copy him. I thought mine would fall out of my face. Then he scratched under his arms like a monkey. All this, I had to mirror. Then we did what Miss Briar called improv. I had to try and sell an object to Roman by only answering questions. So I made my object a bedpan. I held up a sign to the rest of class telling them what my object was and they laughed their heads off, which made me feel good. It was funny. Roman kept asking food-related questions. "Can you eat it?" "Can you eat out of it?" And of course I said, "Only if you're very, very hungry; starving, in fact." Then he asked other questions that made the class roar: "Is it bigger than a bread box?" "Can you sit on it?" To which I said, "Oh, yes." It was pretty hilarious and he never guessed what it was, although he came close. For an hour, I lost myself.

February 1

I started driver's ed. I always thought it would be David who would teach me. He said he would.

Dad says I can drive with him when I get my permit, but, until I get a job, I won't be able to have my own car.

February 4

Dad has been on a baking spree. He bought a cookbook and spends as much time in his kitchen as he used to in the garage. Last week it was a massive chocolate cake with five lopsided layers. Yesterday, he delivered four loaves of sourdough bread. Today, he brought over a cherry pie.

DAD: Kristin, how are you?

ME: Swell, Dad.

DAD: I heard on the news last night about this cult. All of the members assign themselves the role of a certain animal and they take on the animal spirits and speak in tongues: pig tongues, donkey tongues. Doesn't get much weirder than that.

ME: Ig-pay Atin-lay.

DAD: (laughs and snorts at the same time like the dork he is)

ME: I read about a place in Scotland where they grow massive vegetables in the sand.

DAD: What's it called?

ME: Findhorn. It's a spiritual community. I'm going to write and see if I can visit.

DAD: As long as it's not twenty thousand a year.

ME: Thanks loads.

DAD: So, what else is new?

ME: Nothing.

DAD: This is good, you know. Getting together and talking. We talk more now that I've moved out.

ME: You should talk to Mom more.

DAD: I don't know. Maybe after you've been with someone for a long time, you run out of things to say.

ME: Find something you're both interested in.

DAD: Here's something interesting. There's this man

in my building who makes art out of trash. Every day he asks me if I have anything for him.

ME: What, rotting food?

DAD: No. He uses foil, bottle caps, rusty nails. You'd be surprised. And lint. He really likes the stuff left at the bottom of the dryer.

ME: That's weird.

DAD: You'd think, but it's really interesting. I mean it's an invention—his own form of art. When you come, I'll take you to see him.

ME: No, thanks.

DAD: I thought you were adventurous.

ME: Not anymore.

DAD: Sure you are. Did you hear about the man who's living on a billboard on Sunset Boulevard? Seems somebody paid him a quarter million dollars to live on a billboard for six months. He has a sort of cocoon there. And no privacy. Maybe that's the ticket. I'll live in a cocoon on a billboard and make a quarter million dollars.

ME: It's been done now, Dad.

DAD: Well, I could think of something different.

ME: How does he get his food?

DAD: It comes up on an elevator. So, where's your mom today?

ME: In her room, where else?

DAD: Did she know I was coming?

ME: I told her, but I don't get the impression that she hears me.

DAD: She doesn't want to talk to me.

ME: That makes two of us she doesn't want to talk to.

February 6

Being rich isn't all it's cracked up to be, I guess. This rich girl, Patty Hearst, was kidnapped. This would never have happened if her parents had sent her to Swiss boarding school.

February 9

Mom overdoes everything. Because of the gas shortage, she refused to take me to the mall to buy a new bra. I hope I don't end up like one of those women in *Jugs* magazine.

February 15

A valentine from Simon saying that since I've thwarted his advances he's found a more willing victim.

Later: Called Simon about five times. I left messages with his mom, but he hasn't called me back.

*   *   *

February 20

I'm a terrible driver. After I made a right turn over yet another curb, Dad yelled, "Stop the car! Pull over!" He jumped out and just stood on the curb for a while. "Okay," he said, after a few deep breaths.

"Where to, Dad?" I asked as cheerfully as possible.

"The optometrist's," he said. "I think you need glasses."

February 21

Patty Hearst is being held for ransom by the Symbionese Liberation Army, whoever they are. It's pretty weird. They insist that her dad give money to the poor, so I guess it's some kind of Robin Hood thing. Now, if they kidnapped me, I would demand fresh food from restaurants, clean sheets, good books, and color TV.

I hope she comes out okay.

February 22

Listening to Cat Stevens's song, "Sitting": "Life is just a maze of doors and they all / open from the side you're on . . ."

I went to have my eyes checked. Dad was right. I do need glasses. They look kinda good on me, I must admit. Intellectual. Bobby said, "Now we really look like we're related," which I guess he meant as a compliment.

February 25

Woke up to the sound of feet running in the hall. The paramedics took David away again. Bobby rode in the ambulance instead of Mom. "I hope Kristin doesn't wake up," I heard him say to Mom before he left. "She'll be so upset."

It was amazing to me. I do everything possible to demonstrate that I don't get upset. I sat on the stairs and listened to the siren fade away. Then I heard something that shocked me to death. Mom whispering to herself, "Oh God, please let him die."

February 28

David has a kidney infection again. This time, Dad let me go and visit him, so it must be serious. Dad was right: The conditions at the VA hospital are awful. Rows of beds. Some of the men strapped in. Some wandering, mumbling to themselves. The smell of pee. David with an IV in his arm, heavily sedated. His condition is serious, the doctor said, but not critical.

* * *

March 3

I went to a coffee shop with Dad. He talked about his mother. She was fat, but not in a flabby way. She was fat in a hefty way, like a farmer. This is what he remembers about her. Her kitchen presence and the way she expressed love by feeding people. I bit my tongue so I didn't say, "Just like Mom." Instead I asked, "What about your dad?"

"He was skinny as a rail. He had no interest in food and this was the tragedy. He couldn't experience my mother's love without eating her food. But I did. I ate and ate. Mashed potatoes, pie, roast beef, cake, fresh cinnamon bread. I felt loved."

He talked on and on about her: the hats she wore to church with feathers and fruit. "A bird landed on her hat one Sunday and she took it as a compliment from God. 'God likes my hat,' she said. Remember? Remember, Kristin?"

"I don't remember, Dad. She died when I was a baby."

"Yeah. That's right. She did. It's too bad."

"Dad." I broached the subject. "What's going to happen to David?"

"Oh, he'll be all right, I think. Modern medicine. I spoke to the doctor this morning."

"I know, but . . . he's not going to have to go to

the psychiatric ward at that hospital, is he?"

"I hope not, Kristin. I hope not. I wish I could afford to let him stay somewhere nice, somewhere private for a while . . . if only to let your mother have a break. You have no idea how hard it is on her."

"Is that why you split up?"

"I don't know. I used to think that I had a handle on life, that it was simple, you know . . . you did the right thing and . . ." His eyes glazed over for a minute. "Patriotism . . ."

He didn't say anything else.

The silence we all have. Pretending everything will be fine. When it won't. It won't ever be fine again.

March 4

The quiet is eerie. I would welcome the siren, the howling of coyotes or ghosts. Anything. I won't let him end up in the psych ward. I won't!

March 5

Drama is therapeutic, I think, but I'm one awful actress. After I acted my heart out today, Miss Briar said, "Why Kristin, it's the first time I've ever heard Juliet be sarcastic in the balcony scene."

*   *   *

March 6

I spend most of my spare time in the school library.

Yesterday, I met a really nice girl there, from the Philippines. She told me about her life. Her parents are very strict. In the Philippines, when she disobeyed, they would beat her with a stick. To escape, she climbed up the mosquito netting. Here, she says, there is no mosquito netting, so she has to be good.

March 13

David's in a coma. It was all very sudden, the doctor said.

Seeing him so still like that was a shock to all of us, but mostly to Mom. She got so hysterical that the doctor gave her a shot and Bobby had to drive her home.

March 14

I ditched school. No one'll notice. And I can sign Mom's signature perfectly. Waiting. For a miracle, without knowing what would really be miraculous. The doctor said that Mom shouldn't visit the hospital; she's on something that keeps her pretty well knocked out all the time. I'm sad for her, but angry that she just gets to check out, leaving the rest of us to feel.

March 21

Mom found out I've been ditching. Even in her drugged-up state, she insisted I go to school. She wasn't as mad as she usually would be and even wrote a note saying I was sick. I got through the day in a stupor until drama club. For the improv we pretended we were on a sinking ship. Lila Farens, who wears nothing but gray, is an amazing actress. For the entire improv she sobbed at the bottom of the boat, saying, "My poor drowned child. My poor drowned child." It was heartbreaking. I felt like I was going to lose it and cry, so I started making jokes about sharks and piranhas, which made Miss Briar look at me with a sour expression.

Miss Briar talked about how Nixon will probably get away with everything: the lying, the cheating, the spying, and that it'll be so undramatic. Someone should murder Nixon in his sleep, she said. Or we should harken back to the old Westerns and have "a necktie party."

We all looked shocked. "Well, it would make a better play, wouldn't it?" she laughed.

March 22

The girl from the Philippines is named Mia. We sat at a table in the library today, and she told me what life was like before she moved here. Both of her grand-parents died of starvation when something went wrong with their crops. Her mother had two babies born dead. Now, her parents run a small grocery store in South Central L.A., but they live in Glendora so their kids can go to a decent school. Mia says that her parents are afraid that they will be murdered in their store. They've been robbed once. Now they sell the food from the inside of a little cage. It sounds really pathetic.

Mia's writing a book report on *The Diary of Anne Frank.* We looked at Anne's beautiful face on the cover. Then she said, "Death is really slippery; you try to keep in mind the people who are gone, but you can't. They disappear when you grasp for them, and reappear at the strangest moments. Do you believe in ghosts?"

"I don't know," I said. I wanted to tell her about my ghost, but I didn't know how to start.

"I do," she said, "because I've seen the ghosts of my nana and popo (translation—grandma and grandpa). I saw them as if they were alive, looking very confused, when we carried our bags to the ship to leave. Look, I told my mother, there's Nana! My mother got very angry with me and slapped me."

"That's mean."

"I'd upset her." Mia flushed.

It's amazing how different people from other countries are. They speak about real things. All anyone talks about in America are fast cars, boys, girls, makeup, making out.

March 24

We all stood around David in the intensive care ward, all of us but Mom, who was still sedated at home. The doctor asked me to leave.

"Let her stay," Bobby said. His voice sounded old.

Dad pulled me in close.

"A decision needs to be made—" the doctor fiddled with his glasses— "whether you want to continue with life-sustaining measures . . . "

Dad's eyes filled up with tears.

"Of course you don't need to decide anything at this moment or even this day." The doctor's fascination with his glasses made me want to punch him.

"Yes," Dad said, wiping his eyes. "We need time."

None of us talked on the drive home, but when Dad pulled up to the house he said, "Don't tell your mother."

March 28

We've been going over and over the situation:

"Even if he comes out of the coma," Dad said, "his kidneys have stopped functioning. He'll be on dialysis. God knows about his brain." Then he stopped. "Listen, Bobby, Kris, I don't want your opinions. You're too young to have the weight of such decisions."

The larger a star the shorter its life, but all the more fascinating its death. As it collapses within its body, the infalling material can no longer be compressed; the star is blown to pieces; its shattered mass releases outward at the speed of light.

April 2

Mom has been in her room for days. I think of all the times she's been up in the middle of the night, tending to David, her face contorted, her eyes red. I was wrong in what I wrote before. She's felt the anguish for everyone. All along. And I should be nicer to her. We've been like two boats crashing into each other, and I don't know if there's anything I can do to change it. I don't know.

April 3

David could find something to love about anyone. His friend Teddy used to wash his hands over and over again. I haven't seen him lately. Bart Smith had a glass eye, was obsessed with kites. Max Bender was the perfect one, like David, quarterback on the football team, honor student, good-looking. His dad was a doctor and there was a rumor that his dad broke Max's arm when it was time for him to be drafted so he didn't have to go. I've seen Max a couple of times. He works at the record store, but when I look at him, he looks the other way as if he doesn't know me.

April 5

David still in a coma, still on life support. No miracles in this neck of the woods.

April 6

Dad's birthday was pretty sad. Bobby, Michelle, and I stopped at the bookstore and bought a book for him called *Corporate Inventions*. It's filled with stories of guys who were paid a couple hundred bucks for products that made billions for big business. We bought a white cake from the bakery.

It was the first day we didn't visit David.

Dad talked on and on again about his mother's cooking. No one chained her to the kitchen, he says.

She liked it. Her hands covered in flour up to the elbows. Kneading dough, rolling out piecrust, sending him to the fields to pick berries or peaches for her pies. He says the Midwest wasn't so bad. We should move there. There are seasons and no smog. And neighbors. They bring you pies on every occasion . . .

Just as we were leaving, Dad said, "I've made a decision."

We froze.

"No extensive measures . . . ," he said, leaving off the last part of the sentence . . . to keep him alive.

April 10

David died. I can't believe it.

April 13

David's hair was cut. His face clean shaven. He almost looked like himself.

My brother. My brother David.

I thought I would be afraid to approach the open casket, but I wasn't. Bobby and Michelle went first, then Grandma, then Mom, led by Dad. I went last. Before anyone could notice, I slipped my charm bracelet into the pocket of his jacket.

*   *   *

It seemed like the whole town came out. It was if they had awakened after a hundred years, like that town, Brigadoon, in the musical, or Shangri-la.

"Where were all these people when he came back from the war?" Bobby whispered.

Carol and Freddie sat in the row behind us, sobbing, and I couldn't believe that I was ever mad at them for anything. Simon was there with his dad and his sweet mother. She came up to me and squeezed me real tight. O'Neil was there with his pretty wife.

I wanted to pay attention. To watch the coffin without blinking. To hear the priest. But my head felt like a piñata, split open; thoughts tossed everywhere. I thought about the way ribbon frays when it's cut, and how thunder sounds like a drum, and how the women's hats looked like boats on the sea of necks. I thought about how words in the dictionary are cut into parts and the parts amount to nothing by themselves. I thought about the three types of clouds: stratus, cirrus, and cumulus, and how they could be used to describe personalities. The quiet stratus. The fractured cirrus. The creative cumulus, which can look like the bodies of swans and angels and giant stars. David would be a cumulus cloud.

Before I could really focus, the priest was silent, and it was all suddenly over. Over. The casket was closed, the American flag draped over it. Later it was folded and given to Mom and Dad.

The atoms that make up the earth are formed inside of stars. Nothing really dies. Everything is transformed.

PART 3

May 3

I have missed you, blank pages. It's as if I've been held under the water, and have only now come up for air.

What exists beneath the sea?

I'd always pictured it in colors of emerald and aquamarine, where black velvet fish with sequined eyes swim among plankton.

But, when my eyes adjust, I see gray stones, lost anchors, wet wood, buttons, hooks and eyes, the Salem witches who wouldn't float, stars and stripes, missing vessels, wind-up toys, the souls of Romeo and Juliet, peaches, cream, pistons, screams, cages of ribs and birds, tunnels, nutcracker soldiers, satin bows, drug-store signs, Pandora's box ripped open at its hinges.

May 4

Bobby and I have been avoiding each other, the way a sick person avoids the doctor so they won't hear bad news. I think we've been afraid to share our sadness. Tonight, we finally talked.

BOBBY: How's school?

ME: Okay.

BOBBY: It feels pretty endless to me.

ME: You've got it easy.

BOBBY: Yeah, it's easier to be a senior, but . . .

ME: What?

BOBBY: Then it's time to face the future.

ME: Bobby . . . do you believe in life after death?

BOBBY: I don't know. I wish I did.

ME: Yeah. Me, too. Michelle's worried about you.

BOBBY: I know. She's had more awful things in her life than anyone I know, but somehow she manages to be cheerful.

ME: Yeah.

BOBBY: This is really stupid, but last night I dreamt that Michelle was Rapunzel. She was in this huge tower and I was climbing up her hair.

ME: Weird.

BOBBY: But just as I get to the top, I fall and have to start all over again.

ME: Like Sisyphus.

BOBBY: Who's that?

ME: This guy who displeased the gods, and had to push a rock up a hill for eternity, but it was pointless, see, because it just rolled back down again.

BOBBY: It should've been me.

ME: What?

BOBBY: I don't want to be crazy or self-pitying, but I can't get over feeling like it should have been me.

ME: No, Bobby.

BOBBY: David had so many plans, you know? He had a great . . . spirit. I've always just muddled around.

ME: Then why not me? See what I mean? Why not me, then? Or Mom? Or Dad? Or Freddie? It doesn't make sense.

BOBBY: I know. I just can't help feeling like that. Guilty.

ME: It shouldn't have been anybody!

May 5

The school librarian didn't flinch when I told her I wanted to research life after death. I only found one book. It was written by an E.R. doctor. He says that patients who have clinically died and come back to life report traveling through a tunnel of light. It's as if time and space cease to exist and their life is played out before them on a movie screen.

I'll go to St. Agnes tomorrow and speak to the priest.

Later: Bobby looked up his dream in a book of symbols. "Guess what?" he said. "Rapunzel isn't in the book, but a tower is a temenos."

"What's that?" I asked.

"A meeting place with God."

May 6

Going to the church was weird. It made me remember how much I believed in it when I was little. How I used to kneel, open my mouth for the Communion wafer. How awed I was by the pictures along the wall of Jesus suffering.

I kneeled in the confession box. The walls smelled like incense and olive oil. The priest's face appeared behind the dusty screen. Gray-haired, horn-rimmed glasses. Much older than I remembered him. "Yes?" he said. I grasped for the right words. "Bless me, Father, for I have sinned; my last confession was . . ." I couldn't remember. What could I tell him was my sin? That I

wished one day that the ghost would die. That I didn't
do enough to bring David back. That I can't feel anything.

I asked about life after death.

He said he had never known anyone to come back
to life after their death, aside from Jesus. But he had
seen "visitations" at the bedside of someone dying.
Sometimes it was just in the form of a light breeze.
Other times he heard a soft sound, like chimes. Once,
he saw an apparition—a white fog swirled into shape
before his eyes.

Suddenly, he became abrupt. As if he thought I
was playing a joke on him.

PRIEST: This isn't why you're supposed to come here.
    You're supposed to come here for your sins.

ME: I did come here for my sins.

PRIEST: What are they, then?

ME: There's too many of them.

PRIEST: You're too young to have too many.

ME: I don't feel anything. I'm all numb inside.

PRIEST: I see. What's the weather like out there?

ME: The weather?

PRIEST: Are you a parrot? (I didn't answer.) No, you're
    not a parrot. You're a little girl, aren't you?

ME: If you call fifteen little.

PRIEST: Pop your head out of this box for a second. Who do you see in the church?

ME: Just a few women.

PRIEST: Young or old?

ME: Old, mostly.

PRIEST: So, comparatively speaking, you're a little girl.

ME: I guess.

PRIEST: Well, I'll tell you a secret. They're little girls, too. You look past those wrinkles, beneath their hats and gray hair and they're children. But the men! The real sinners! Do they ever come? Never. It's women who feel guilty. I blame it on the story of Eve. See my point?

ME: I guess.

PRIEST: Is it still cloudy outside? The forecast said there's a storm.

ME: I don't believe in God.

PRIEST: God is like the weather. Whether you believe in Him or not, it's still gonna rain. The problem with you Californians is that you always have sunny weather. So you don't have to think about God. I spent most of my life in upstate New York, and believe me, they have weather. And they believe in God. Look at this place. This confession *box*. It's like a coffin. How would you like to spend a lot of time here? And why do I? Women.

Women and their guilt. Do you put yourself to use?

ME: Sometimes. Not lately, I guess.

PRIEST: If it's still windy out there, my tomatoes will get spoiled. Maybe you'll check on them. They're in the little patio behind the church. Also, stack the patio chairs and put them in the cubby on their sides. See, if you use your time productively, you'll sin less.

ME: Alright.

PRIEST: But first you have to do your penance. Ten Hail Marys.

ME: But . . .

PRIEST: And tell all those women out there to put themselves to good use.

ME: But I haven't told you my sin.

PRIEST: What is your sin?

ME: I—

PRIEST: It doesn't matter what it was. The point is . . . will you do it again?

ME: I don't know.

PRIEST: Ten Hail Marys, as I said. And throw in the Lord's Prayer for good measure.

The wind was blowing hard outside. When I got to his tomatoes, several of the pots were knocked over, but the tomatoes were intact. I carried the pots into a small shed, then restaked the vines. Within minutes, thunder came, then rain.

I was putting myself to use.

May 10

We celebrated Bobby's birthday in pieces. Mom left a wrapped package on the table for him: a jigsaw puzzle suitable for a twelve-year-old. Dad took him to a baseball game. I had found this really cool pipe at the head shop. It looks like a Greek god's head carved out of wood. Of course, Bobby doesn't smoke, but it's a cool thing anyway. Then, since we're all practically broke, Michelle and I took him to McDonald's, where we ate flat little tasteless hamburgers (aka cardboard sandwiches).

May 11

Dad got a job at the bakery. On weekends, he bakes breads and pastries. During the week, he paints houses. At night, he calls with his crazy news stories:

DAD: I read about Siamese twins who were joined together at the head. When one of them got married, the other had to go along for the ride. It was like polygamy. They interviewed the nonmarried twin and she said she doesn't even feel jealous about her sister's marriage. She sleeps on a shelf that slides out from the marriage bed and just closes her eyes real tight when things get, well, marital. The interviewer asked her what would happen if she got married. She said, "We'll have to either all live together or take turns living in one house or the other." Imagine that.

ME: What newspaper do you read?

DAD: Oh, I read all of them, while the dough is rising.

ME: I have a question.

DAD: Shoot.

ME: If Mom wanted you to move back into the house, would you do it?

DAD: I never wanted to move out in the first place. I love your mom.

Now all I have to do is convince her.

Called Grandma several times. She can actually be a comfort. She expresses her real feelings more than the rest of us. After the funeral, when we all sat around like mannequins, she put her face in the flag and sobbed for about three hours. She felt for all of us that day.

She wasn't home, though. Probably out with Italo.

*   *   *

P.S. I prayed last night. Please don't tell anyone. Of course you won't, because books don't talk (unless someone finds them!).

Just in case, I prayed. That David's soul is in heaven and that someday I'll join him.

May 12

Had a nightmare that I was joined at the head with David. Every time he moved, I had to move, and vice versa.

May 13

Carol and Freddie eloped in Vegas. She says they're legally married! They've rented an apartment behind McDonald's with the money Freddie saved from working at Tastee-Freez. He's dropped out of school and will be the manager there now.

ME: But the ice cream there is so bad; it tastes like air.

CAROL: But that's not the point, Kristin. Really, you're so silly. We're in the real world now. Like grown-ups.

ME: What's so great about being grown up?

CAROL: Everything! Aren't you happy for me?

ME: (lying) Of course. How're the ol' parents taking it?

CAROL: They're happy as clams. My dad has always wanted to get rid of me and now Mom can leave

and find some jockey to marry and move to Peru
or wherever the jockeys are from.

I don't know. I guess I should be happy for her.
But the whole thing makes me sick to my stomach.

May 14

I saw Mia today. "It's been very bad at my house,"
she said. "My brother has joined up with a gang. My
father made him stay home last night by pointing a
gun at him. When my father fell asleep, my brother
stole the gun from him. He says he'll kill my father if
he tries to stop him from being in the gang. He says
my father knows nothing about power and progress
in America. Slaving away gets you nothing but old.
My father has changed all the locks on our doors and
put bars on the windows. My brother is no longer one
of the family. He has acted disrespectfully. I cannot
mention his name." Mia sounded so sad that I was
speechless. "He used to be my best friend in the world.
Now, he is nothing."

We have more in common than she knows.

May 16

Went over to Carol and Freddie's "place" for dinner. It seems her mom has given her a new cookbook that she wants to try out. The apartment is even grimier than Dad's. Most of the gross furniture in Tracey's house was transferred to Carol: the Formica table with red flecks, the matching red vinyl chairs, the Naugahyde couch with heart-shaped pillows, the prints of sad children with huge eyes.

Carol seemed very nervous. "Now that Freddie has a big job," she said, "he expects so much of me."

"Really? I thought he was so stoned all the time that he didn't notice anything." Out it came. Sarcasm. But C. didn't seem to notice.

"He doesn't smoke anymore. He says he needs to be responsible. Maybe that's the problem. And he wants me to act like a 'wife.'"

That word made me shudder. "Wife." Yech. Just as we were deep in this discussion, smoke poured in from the kitchen. "The roast!" Carol hadn't unwrapped it before putting it in the oven!

After we dragged the thing out and opened the windows, Carol sank to the floor and cried. "Freddie will be so mad at me."

God, it gave me the heebie-jeebies.

*   *   *

I pedaled to the store and bought a couple of steaks and showed her how to broil them. Fortunately, Freddie had to work late, so I was spared the new, improved version of him.

May 17

Returned to drama club, for the first time since David died. "I lit a candle so you could find your way," Miss Briar said, hugging me. I tried to think of something smart to say, but nothing came to mind.

Miss Briar keeps going on and on about the need for catharsis in acting and in life. She was impressed by what she calls my newfound talent. "You've gone from acting everything with sarcasm to acting with authenticity. Honestly, your Ophelia made me want to jump right into the river with you."

After drama, I met Gloria downtown for a Coke. She said that the baby is coming to live with her. "I don't really hate her guts, Kristin. I love her." Her mother will watch the baby while Gloria is at school. "It's time I take responsibility for my life," she said. Then she talked about all of the atrocities that go on right in front of our eyes, like how her parents are treated so shabbily just because they're different. She's becoming "an activist," which made me feel really self-centered because all I think about are my own tragedies. She's almost finished with her documentary, which she's making with some students at U.S.C.

Saw Simon with his "girlfriend," Cathy. It's a little hard not to feel jealous. I mean, if I was going to have a boyfriend, Simon would be my choice. He's pretty much the smartest kid I know.

May 20

Bobby got a job at Carrow's waiting tables. "Gross," I said. "How can you be like a servant?"

"I made fifty dollars in tips," he said. "I'll take you to Las Vasquelas for dinner."

"Cool." If he's going to spend it on me, who am I to criticize where he gets it?

Is it a sin that life goes on?

It has no choice but to go on.

May 21

When I asked Mom what she thinks about

Grandma having a boyfriend, she said, "She can't have a boyfriend. She's my mother. Is this an April Fool's joke?"

"Mom," I said. "This is May."

"It doesn't matter what month it is, Kristin. What matters is that she was a terrible mother. I had to figure out how to be a mother on my own. It wasn't so hard with the boys. They just played and got dirty and I washed their clothes. But you! That's another story."

"I'm sorry I've been so difficult," I said. I meant it to be sincere, but it came out sounding sarcastic.

As if she was in her own conversation, Mom said, "I just can't believe that after all these years of moping about my dad, she's finally seeing someone." Then she opened the fridge and closed it: "God, Kris, you've gotten thin. How do you stay that way? But of course, it's your age." I thought she might realize then that she never cooks dinner anymore. Does she think it's supposed to appear automatically?

"Mom, let's go out to dinner, okay? We can splurge just this once. You haven't been anywhere in weeks."

"I thought California was the land of milk and honey, but it's not. And the insects here! Especially spiders. Spiders love hot weather."

For days she has not said one word to me, then this.

May 23

A boy I don't know walked up to me at school. "If you're an American outside the bathroom, what are you inside?"

"I don't know," I said.

"You're a peein'." (European) Weird.

May 26

Carol asked me to come over today and when I got to her apartment, the door was wide open, so any of the drunks who live in her complex could just wander in. Carol fixed me a cup of coffee, which I can't stand, but drank.

CAROL: Are you doing okay?

ME: Yeah.

CAROL: Gosh, It's such a sad year, Kris. I mean, with David dying. I always thought he'd get better and stuff.

ME: I guess we all thought so.

CAROL: Yeah.

ME: Are you okay?

CAROL: I'm okay. My mom is looking for a new husband. She says she wants to marry a doctor because they make more money, so she keeps pretending to be sick. She's sticking with the pig until she finds one, though.

ME: It's weird. Your parents are the ones who should separate, not mine.

CAROL: Yeah.

ME: Your mom and my mom never go out anymore.

CAROL: My mom says your mom isn't any fun.

ME: Oh. So how come you haven't been in school?

CAROL: I'm going to drop out, I guess.

ME: Why?

CAROL: Freddie thinks I should. He thinks we should have two incomes.

ME: I don't think you should.

CAROL: But I'm not smart like you. I flunked two years, remember? There isn't really any point in my going.

ME: You've gone for eleven years, or however many. You might as well finish.

CAROL: (starting to cry) I kinda miss the kids. This feels like the end of my life.

ME: It's not!

CAROL: You know what? I don't like Freddie. I used to like him. But now I don't.

ME: So, what's changed?

CAROL: I used to like him when he was stoned, you know? He was funny and easy to get along with. Now he's all "responsible" and he nags at me all the time.

ME: I'm sorry.

CAROL: My life stinks.

ME: Why don't you just move home?

CAROL: I can't.

ME: Why not? You've made it through this many years.

CAROL: I can't stand the idea of going back there to live. Maybe someone could put me up for auction.

ME: What do you mean?

CAROL: You know, in the old days, how they'd auction off slaves? They'd put them up on a stage with a rope around their neck. Peel back their lips to show their teeth. Then someone would buy them.

ME: I don't get it.

CAROL: My teeth are good. I've never even had a cavity. If they put me up on the auction block, someone could take me. And my chances would be fifty-fifty that they'd treat me right.

ME: I don't think they'd be fifty-fifty, Carol. But you know, it does make me think that arranged marriages might be a good idea.

CAROL: Yeah, who would my dad pick for me?

ME: Good point.

CAROL: Last night I saw a *Twilight Zone* where these guys come back from a mission and they disappear one by one. They're in a hospital and then there's one less bed, until the last guy calls his parents and tells them he's their son and they don't even say he's dead, Kristin. They say that he never existed. They never had a son, right? And then he disappears.

May 28

I feel so bad for Carol. To choose between Freddie and the fascist. Still, if she goes home, she'll get to leave eventually. If she stays with Freddie and drops out of school . . .

I wish she could live with us, but Mom is too wigged-out as it is.

May 29

Racking my brains about C. I used to think in my misguided way, that everyone had the same chances, that everyone could make something of their lives if they only had the will. But Carol may be right. She has no defenses, and (sadly) she's not too bright.

I asked Bobby what he thought.

BOBBY: Kristin, you know how I'm going to end up?

ME: What?

BOBBY: A stuffed shirt.

ME: What do you mean?

BOBBY: I can feel it. Maybe I'll even become a Republican!

ME: A Republican and a dentist! That's way too weird.

BOBBY: Well, I won't go that far. Maybe.

ME: Promise?

BOBBY: What I mean is that I can see that just about everything has to do with money. And I'm just going to have to make that my focus.

ME: What does this have to do with Carol?

BOBBY: Well, as I see it, Carol's probably never going to make much money on her own. So, she needs to marry well. Money doesn't seem important to her now, but it will later.

ME: I don't think money gives you happiness.

BOBBY: It helps.

ME: So, you think she should go back to her parents?

BOBBY: Yeah, and I think she should try to marry someone with more potential than Freddie. She's got to consider her assets and build on them.

ME: What are her assets?

BOBBY: Looks, to a certain extent. And sweetness. But she has the flaw of choosing the wrong type. She'll have to get over that.

ME: At least we agree on something.

*　　　*　　　*

Bobby is so weird. As much as I want him to be, he'll never be like David. David would have persuaded Mom to take Carol in; I just know it. He loved to give advice. I remember the time Eddie Kitz accidently set the school on fire. He and his friends were launching model rockets, and one flew into the window and started the trash on fire. Eddie's dad was really mean, like the fascist, and Eddie was worried what would happen. David actually went to the school principal with Eddie to explain.

Eddie had to clean lockers for the rest of the school year, but I don't think the principal told his dad.

David would have helped Carol figure things out.

May 30

All night, a storm. The sound of the wind reminded me of the ghost, that stranger. As weird as it sounds, I think I miss him, too. The ghost never took me to Disneyland, or tried to teach me to put the basketball through the hoop, but he was here, making noise, trying to say something that none of us could understand. Now, I'll never know him and I'll never know if David would have made it into space, or been an astronomer, or a doctor, or all of the dreamy things he wanted to be and do.

Later: Knocked the stuff off my dresser: the statues, bottles of cologne, papers, everything. Threw my trash can against the wall. Ripped the curtains off my windows. No one noticed. Now any weirdo who wants to can look in my window and watch me.

Who cares?

May 31

Bobby took me out and bought me a bathing suit. It's got a tiger pattern, with netting on the sides. Way cool. As we were leaving May Company, he put his arm around me. He's never done that. "I'll always take care of you," he said. "Even if I become a Republican."

June 1

Italo is moving in with Grandma! Grandma says it'll save money for both of them. Besides, she thinks that marriage takes the umph out of a relationship. Italo's photograph has replaced my mother's on top of the TV. Now my mother as a little girl—double braided, freckled—stares up at me from a shelf in the kitchen. I call that picture of Mom "Little Girl Lost." Italo's photograph is different—a thin face, a long elegant beak, gray hair, grinning teeth; the kind of person that twirls spaghetti around a fork, the kind that sings at all sorts of inopportune moments.

∗　　　∗　　　∗

Grandma has dyed her hair chestnut brown (she says "Clairol has worked wonders in my life"). She's opened the windows of her apartment and replaced the old lace curtains with peach seashells on a sea of burgundy and green. Instead of blaring the TV, she plays "Rhapsody on a Theme of Paganini" on the hi-fi. She looks about twenty years younger.

People can change.

Later: Went with Simon and Cathy to a Fellini movie. If Fellini doesn't portray reality, who does? All these crazy people milling about in Rome. It's like Fellini sees the weirdness inside of people and turns them inside out for the movie. Afterwards, Cathy asked, "Why do they put those words at the bottom of the screen?"

"Those are subtitles, Cathy." Simon sounded grouchy.

"What for?"

"So you can read what they're saying."

"Ohhh," she said, with sudden insight.

She's a real bright one, alright. A match made in heaven.

June 4

Carol moved back in with her parents. What's that phrase? "Out of the frying pan, into the fire." O'Neil arranged for her to be readmitted to school, even though it's the last week. It'll take her an extra semester now. "I'll be a million years old when I graduate," she said.

I asked if she would continue seeing Freddie. "Not if I can help it," she said. "I don't want to grow up so fast."

I've been telling her that all along.

June 5

Mom is obsessed with spiders. She roots around in corners, behind the refrigerator, under the beds, with the end of a wire hanger. When they make a run for it, she's ready with an old rolled-up copy of *Reader's Digest* or *Life*. Gray ones, harmless bolas spiders, it doesn't matter. To her they are all black widows.

ME: Mom, maybe you need to go back to your shrink.

MOM: You yourself know very well that psychiatrists are crazy.

ME: True.

MOM: Besides which, that idiot is the one who told me to leave your father.

ME: So tell Dad to come back.

MOM: Your dad hates spiders. He would never come back.

June 6

"What was Mom like when she was my age?" I ask Grandma, who is putting on false eyelashes. If I wanted to play a dirty trick, I would leave those on my mother's pillow—they look like bisected spiders.

GRANDMA: Sullen. She moped around the house and looked at me like I'd done something wrong to her, like it wasn't her father who deserted us, but me who had driven him away.

ME: I should do something . . . hire an exterminator or something; even the ants look like spiders to Mom.

GRANDMA: We'll ask Italo. He knows everything.

ME: When am I going to meet Italo?

GRANDMA: Soon. Soon. That's a very big step, introducing the boyfriend to the family. It makes a statement, you know. I'm afraid your mother might be rude to him.

Grandma is such a character.

Later: Mia called. She and her family are moving to San Francisco. She wouldn't say why, but it's got to be because of her crazy brother. Can't life just stay still for once? She said, "Thank you for being my friend. I hope we'll see each other again." I cried for about an hour. I found myself praying that things will work out for her. I surprised myself; it's been a while since I really prayed like that.

June 6

Crazy! Patty Hearst is kidnapped, held hostage, probably brainwashed, then dragged on a bank robbery. And she's charged with the crime. Meanwhile, Nixon continues to go scot-free.

June 7

Gloria showed her film in the library auditorium. It was so fantastic, I can't even express it. It was a documentary on a group of men who live on the streets in downtown L.A. She interviews them, but the camera never leaves their faces. They're talking about their lives before they became homeless. About two-thirds of them are Vietnam veterans. Then, she spliced together quick shots of all the faces so that they seem to blur together. Suddenly, the interest is lost; you care less about them because they're a mass. They become easily ignored.

*   *   *

If David hadn't had us, he could have been any of them.

June 9

just before dark, I walked up Glendora Mountain Road. The hills, the valley, the sky, are so beautiful. I want to capture this nature somehow. I want to chisel at the infrastructures of the minutest botanical and astronomical forms, and understand—everything.

At the top, I turned toward Pirate's Cove. The road there veers off suddenly. If someone turns wrong, they wind up in the canyon. There are pieces of car down at the bottom.

I envisioned the ghosts—the teenagers who have driven off the road to their deaths. Not all of them died. Jimmy Johnson was paralyzed in '71, after he drove his motorcycle off; you can still see him rolling around town in his wheelchair with a can of Colt 45 in his lap. Sarah Bedding walked away without a scratch after her MG tumbled down. Most of them died, though. I grew up with all of these people, but hardly knew any of them.

June 11

Mom asked the oven, "Why don't you keep me warm at night, you jerk?"

"Maybe if you cook something in it, it will," I said, but she just walked away like she didn't hear me.

Later: School is out, which is not something I've looked forward to. Too much time on my hands.

For years I've wanted ultimate freedom, to be able to come and go as I pleased. Now I have it because nobody really cares what I do. It's not all it's cracked up to be. Even driving is a disappointment. A.) Mom hardly ever lets me use the car. B.) There's no place to go.

June 12

When I visit Dad, it's like visiting Grandma used to be—the radio news hums in the background and Dad is off while he talks with me, fiddling with a contraption, picking the paint flecks from his hands. There's always a stack of goodies from the bakery, at least. It's better than starving at home.

DAD: How's your mother doing?

ME: She talks to the appliances.

DAD: A person needs someone to talk to, I guess.

ME: I think she's going batty.

*   *   *

Dad lit a cigarette and I thought the subject was dropped. Then he worked on this gadget—a measuring scale that has all kinds of interchangeable tables in all shapes and sizes for people who measure their foods, "for dieters."

DAD: She feels she's to blame.

ME: For what?

DAD: You know, for David's death. She says it's her fault, that she "wished it on him." It's crazy, I know. But there's no making it right. Listen, Kristin, why don't you work weekends at the bakery with me? I'll teach you how to make bread. You'll want to start saving for college soon. God knows I won't be much help to you now that I'm paying for these two households.

ME: Sure, Dad. I better go.

I biked home as fast as I could. Mom was sitting at the table with the crumpled want ads and old photo albums. The photos were of her and Dad. Mom in a white dress and matching pumps waving for the camera. Mom at Knott's Berry Farm sitting on a bench next to a statue of a cowboy. Mom smiling. But her eyes still have the same look as the photo at Grandma's: Little Girl Lost. She showed me a picture of me as a baby. She is holding me, her mouth open, her head cocked.

ME: What are you doing in that picture?

MOM: Singing.

ME: Remember what you were singing?

MOM: (sings) Six little ducks went out to play . . . over the hills and far away . . . the little one says quack quack quack quack . . . but only (Her voice fades off, and she turns the page.)

ME: Mom . . . I need to talk to you.

MOM: I don't have time.

ME: It's important.

MOM: Can't you see I'm job hunting?

ME: Please.

MOM: Look, I've circled enough for both of us.

ME: Mom! I felt the way you did! I wished that David would die. It wasn't him anymore. And Dad said they shouldn't try to keep him alive. And all of us knew it was right. It wasn't anybody's fault!

She stared at me in that blank way she does, then her face just crumpled up and she started crying. Then I started crying and neither of us could stop.

Later: Woke up at 3:00 A.M. and crept into David's room. I talked to David about the ghost who came to

live in his body, the sad soul who was taken back into
the earth.

David's trophies are dusty again.

I felt him there with me. The real David. My David.
David, you are still here. Alive. Alive in me.
Alive in the galaxy.
Alive in the stars.
Alive in the sky.
Alive in the sea.
Alive in the palm trees.
Alive in feathers.
Alive in birds.
Alive in the mountains.
Alive in the coyotes.
Alive in books.
Alive in sound.
Alive in Mom.
Alive in Dad.
Alive in Bobby.
Alive in me.
Alive in soil.
Alive in branches.
Alive in fossils.

Alive in tongues.
Alive in eyes.
Alive in cries.
Alive in bodies.
Alive in past, present, future.
Alive forever.

June 13

I woke up this morning to a pleasant surprise: the smell of bacon and eggs, coffee, pancakes. Mom had bought groceries and made a big breakfast for us. Bobby came downstairs, looked at the table and said, "Is it a holiday?"

Maybe it is.

June 25

Simon came over. We listened to Simon and Garfunkel.

ME: Garfunkel's voice is sweeter.

SIMON: Simon's got the poetry in his voice, though, the nuances. Besides, he writes the music. He's got my name after all. Kristin?

ME: What?

SIMON: I'm sorry for acting like an idiot all year. I've acted like . . .

ME: Like a male chauvinist . . .

SIMON: Yes.

ME: Like an adolescent brat . . .

SIMON: That's right. And with everything you were going through . . .

ME: Well . . . you've got Cathy now . . .

SIMON: I broke up with her. (He looked at his feet.) I feel really mean about it, but something snapped. I don't know. It's like I had forgotten everything I believed. I guess I've grown up a little. I was acting like a moron. It's embarrassing.

ME: You have grown . . . about two feet, Simon!

SIMON: I mean, inside. You know.

ME: I know what you mean.

SIMON: I still think you're beautiful.

ME: Let's not start that again.

SIMON: I just want it for the record.

ME: Turn the record over!

SIMON: Let's make a pact that we'll go to the same college.

ME: I won't be able to afford a college you'll go to.

SIMON: Then I'll go to a state college.

ME: Okay. What are you going to be this week?

SIMON: Kristin, be nice.

ME: It's not my nature.

SIMON: It is so your nature.

ME: I think I'll study astronomy.

SIMON: I'll probably study art history like my old man.

ME: Don't sound so happy about it!

SIMON: It's just that it bugs me that I'm so much like him. I mean, I really get excited about this stuff, and I'm not talented enough to actually be an artist. Besides, I know as much about art as anybody.

ME: That's true.

SIMON: This song's my favorite.

ME: Mine, too.

SIMON: I love that line, "I don't know a dream that's not been shattered / Or driven to its knees."

ME: When we were little we mixed our blood, do you remember that?

SIMON: Let's do it again.

ME: No! Gross!

SIMON: Come on.

ME: Uh-uh. Let's think of something else.

SIMON: Our saliva?

ME: You promised.

SIMON: Well, what?

ME: Something we can do in memory of David.

SIMON: Okay. I guess we're old enough to start making some kind of impression on the world.

ME: We have to start sometime.

July 1

Bobby, Michelle, Simon, and I went to Newport Beach. We swam in the ocean (which was freezing) and had ice cream and Bobby did all these dorky tricks like posing as a muscle man. Then we ate at Denny's and talked about putting up a plaque at the high school, to honor the students who died in the war.

July 4

Tonight we all gathered to celebrate Mom's birthday and Independence Day. It was Grandma's idea. Bobby, Dad, Mom, Michelle, Simon, Grandma, and (finally) Italo and I got together at our house for a barbecue. For once, we ate well. Italo barbecued salmon and chicken in Italian vinegar. Mom made salad with real (not iceberg) lettuce. Dad made a flag cake. Michelle brought brownies. We lit sparklers and Roman candles. Simon brought these cool black pellets that turn into snakes. I actually felt happy for once, as if time, caught in a bottomless ditch, had suddenly lurched forward, was moving again.

Italo is very philosophical. The opposite of my long lost grandfather, Morton, the practical joker. It's interesting how Morton deserting Grandma impacted so many different lives. Like a row of dominoes.

*   *   *

Italo's a real talker. He went on and on about love. At one point he said, "Devotion is not just roses and champagne. Devotion is cleaning someone's bedpan. Or standing by them when everyone else thinks they're wrong. It's making tough decisions on their behalf."

When he said that, Dad gave Mom a meaningful look, but she was too busy trying to open the bottle of wine to notice. It'll be an uphill battle, if they're ever going to get back together. Dad said that he can't afford two households much longer, even with the extra job. What a romantic! But! They celebrated the holiday together. And he bought her a really nice necklace made with freshwater pearls (the cheap kind). So, at least that's something.

July 30

Nixon will be impeached. Rumor has it that he'll resign. At last. It's gone on so long it feels like the whole country has been holding its breath. This whole era behind us. Dad says the country will never be the same.

August 4

I'm at the park behind the school with Mom. It's

the first nice day we've had in weeks, what with the smog. Everyone is out in full force: teenagers, women with their babies, children with jump ropes and hula hoops, old men with their newspapers.

The sky is hot. Mom's arms are already turning pink. There's no wind. The birds are chirping. A sparrow flies away from her nest about a foot, then flies back again. Another dives down to pick up dried pine needles. I like the way birds make their nests from anything they find. I've heard that mockingbirds are so unafraid of humans that they will pluck the hair right off your head. Woven in with grass, stippled with old gum wrappers, twigs, shreds of nature, the hair adds the final strength to their homes.

It's the same with humans, I guess. Out of the scraps and debris and the beautiful things, we build our lives. As Simon would say, it takes "imagination."

David and I used to go behind the hedges, to this old fence covered with grapevines. If it was the right season we would eat the ripe, plump grapes. David had a way of doing things he wasn't exactly supposed to, without making it seem wrong. Once, when the man who lived behind the park yelled at us for eating his grapes, David said sweetly, "But they're so delicious. Who could resist?" The man launched into a lecture about growing grapes and gave us bags to take some home.

I learned to question the rules from David.

In the evening, David and I would watch the sky, trying not to blink until the stars appeared suddenly, like bright ghosts. "How'd you like to be up there in a spaceship?" David would say. "I really think that's the future." He wanted to build floating cities, massive vessels that would contain small worlds in space. But I couldn't imagine being contained like that, in a capsule, no matter how large. I couldn't imagine not being able to run as far and fast as I wanted to without falling off of the edge of something.

What I could see was our bodies in the sky, unencumbered. No space stations. Or rockets. Or cities on the moon.

Just our bodies, like birds, soaring through those galaxies.